HELIX

HELIX

Graeme Bennett

Published by Graeme Bennett Ltd.

CONTENTS

CONTENTS

Preface

Is math's ability to plot vectors, express irrational numbers and smooth curves to approximate the fullness of pure analog expression close enough to matter? What if, in a pure analog reality, there's an 'ingredient x' that defies digital approximation—at least until a new mathematical approach opens the door?

It's this new approach—all based on a single, surprisingly literal reinterpretation of Einstein's theory of space-time—that drives our story.

As the plot develops, we witness a future in which bio-augmentation leads to intelligence augmentation, creating a significant culture gap between those who have these "upgrades" and those who do not.

This is not the AI-enhanced and workforce automation-driven future of prosperity we were promised! This is a world where these tools have already displaced many in low-skilled occupations and the trend continues to accelerate. We see how AI-led development environments, self-driving vehicles, robotic manufacturing facilities, and other "smart" technologies disrupt increasing numbers of career categories, and how a backlash might develop.

Our characters explore the paradoxical relationship between quantum field theory and general relativity—and how math alone cannot fully describe the analog world.

These ideas are the vehicle in which this story travels to its far-flung destinations across time and space.

Enjoy the ride.
Graeme Bennett
November 16, 2023

Prologue

The atmosphere was suddenly energized as an electromagnetic hum became tangible. The faint whine increased in intensity and a researcher at a nearby desk felt the hairs on his arms bristle as the system neared peak power. The clock on the wall read 3:05. As the second hand advanced, the time suddenly jumped forward 17 seconds.

Excerpts from the HELX Lectures

Two weeks earlier

The young professor stood at the podium in the lecture hall, his energetic voice echoing in the mostly-empty room. A dozen or so students sat in the seats closest to him taking notes; a few others sat closer to the exit doors.

"...The practical reality we are now facing is that the two leading scientific theories as to the nature of space-time are at odds with each other. They cannot both be correct. Our fundamental concepts of space-time were shaped in the early 20th century by Einstein, Bohr and Heisenberg (to name just a few), just as our notions about the foundations of classical mechanics were shaped by Newton in the 17th century."

He raised his hands, his voice rising. "Now, emerging cosmological theories are beginning to question some of these long-held notions and new experimental results from CERN,

Brookhaven, and other facilities around the world are providing answers to questions that many scientists hadn't even thought to ask. *Your* generation's greatest scientific legacy may be your contribution to finally fitting together the missing pieces of the puzzle that reveals the true and essential nature of reality itself."

The professor paused, as the screen flipped from a photo of the Large Hadron Collider to one of a spiral galaxy. "Questions?"

A young woman with long reddish-blonde hair in the second row raised her hand first, followed by several others. The professor gestured to the young woman.

"Uh, Susan, in the second row?"

"Professor Rutherford, are you familiar with the work on Cherenkov radiation being done by Dr. Erich Rössler and his team?"

Rutherford smiled. "Yes, I'm one of the reviewers of their latest paper on quantum field theory, and I'm following their progress on the HELX—the high energy large accelerator—with great interest." He smiled at the class and rubbed his hands together comically. "Well, Susan, have you got any news for us?"

Susan smiled and nodded. "I do, actually. I've just been invited to join the HELX team working on the experimental side. In field equations."

Rutherford stepped out from behind the podium and stepped down off its raised platform. "That's wonderful news, isn't it class?"

Amid scattered applause, someone said "Woot" and a few people chuckled.

As the room fell back into the usual rustling noises, Professor Rutherford glanced down at his speaking notes. "Indeed, congratulations," he said, looking at her over the top of his glasses. "I hear they've just had a bit of a breakthrough over there."

Susan smiled. "I've been told that it's not supposed to be officially announced until the peer reviews are complete, but yes, it looks encouraging."

"Well thank you for sharing your good news. Perhaps you can tell me at little more about this offline? I'd be happy to speak to you immediately following the Q&A."

"Certainly, Professor—thank you."

"Next question?"

A petite Indian woman sitting near the center of the first row raised her hand. Professor Rutherford pointed to her with his rolled-up speaking notes. "Yes, Indra?"

"Can you tell us a little more about the recent changes at the accelerator facility?"

"Well, I must confess I was a little surprised today at what showed up in my inbox from the nice folks on the HELX team."

That caught everyone's attention. The room suddenly became very quiet. He began slowly.

"So far, the facility's been very open with sharing its results. Although, like any good research center, they are careful not to jump to conclusions or make, you know, unsubstantiated claims. Even so, it has never been quite as hush-hush as it might be if the university hadn't been involved—if it had belonged from the start to a private research group, or, say a military-funded thing."

Was he playing up the sense of apprehension? If so, it was convincing. Menacing, almost. He paced the floor, then returned to the microphone at the podium.

"And so I get this letter today. And hey, I'm suddenly being asked to sign a non-disclosure agreement."

A few muttered 'boos' rose from the silence like a mumbling soundtrack.

"So, I suppose this means they're onto something. Or perhaps they're just 'adulting' at being a corporation; I don't know." He exhaled rather heavily into the microphone. "This, then, will probably be the last full-disclosure report I can give you...."

He glanced in Susan's direction and smiled faintly.

"It also means my sources probably haven't told me the good stuff yet. Anyway..."

He paused for a second; the whispering ceased almost immediately.

"For the most part, the math they're using is pretty well understood—field equations and so on. It's just the way it has been applied, it's kind of a unique 'field array' approach to generate dynamic field effects, phase shifts, quantum wave resonance, and that sort of thing."

He gestured toward the screen. "A lot of these topics are being explored in cosmology, quantum physics, medicine and so on, but it's kind of unique for a research facility to be pulling them all together like this."

He shut off the projector's lamp, then glanced at the wall-clock and turned it on again. "I'll be just a few seconds," he announced to his now-curious audience. He pulled up a HELX presentation from the department's intranet site. "I might not be allowed to mention this again later, so here's what I *do* know."

The image changed from an exterior shot of the facility to a view of an imposing circular structure, bristling with cables, pipes and control surfaces.

"For those who don't know, MPAX—or MPACTD as it was previously known—is a large-scale facility in the southeast corner of the Research Quadrangle housing the massive particle accelerator and collider/synchrotron known as HELX. Although housed on university lands, it now operates as a public company—an independent spinoff of the Research Campus of Princeton University, operating as a for-profit commercial entity, with its own corporate sponsors and a separate board of directors. The facility got its start as a government-backed research project for testing M-Theoretical Particle Asymmetry Corresponding to T-Duality. The original, single-magnet accelerator was decommissioned just last year when the new facility opened on Highway 1, about four miles from here and the project was spun off to the AIMG group that now owns and manages it."

The on-screen image changed to show the new, more impressive-looking, building.

"This new project is home to the world's first quantum harmonic oscillator accelerator, which is essentially a large-scale quantum wave generator and wave function collapsor. If you look up *T-Duality*, you'll get a basic idea of what they're aiming for over there. If you're interested in the math—which is very interesting, I might add—take a look at the quantum representation of *Momentum Space*, in particular *Pontryagin duality*."

He wrote the latter phase on the whiteboard.

"Or," he said with a wink, "you could probably ask Susan in a week or two."

He glanced again at the clock, then turned off the lamp on the projector and retracted the projection screen, As it rolled up out of sight, the professor wrote out an example on the whiteboard. "Okay, here's our equation of the day."

""Here's a three-dimensional wave function in momentum space...." He drew an oval around the equation. "For Monday: how can we generalize this as a weighted sum of orthogonal basis functions?"

He erased the contents of the board around the oval and pointed to the equation with the eraser to emphasize his words. "Also for Monday, tell me *why* the momentum in this equation doesn't have a fixed value—and be prepared to discuss."

He looked at the clock. "Okay, that's all the time we have for today."

After the lecture, Susan approached the podium as the professor was gathering up his notes. "Can you come back to the classroom with me?" he asked.

"Sure," she said.

They walked together into the bustling hall and reached

the professor's office just as the last student closed the door to the adjacent classroom.

"Go on in," he said. "I'll be there in a moment."

She poked her head tentatively into the empty classroom, then went in. She set her backpack down on the floor next to the front desk and stood there, contemplating the posters on the walls near the door.

One of the posters said, *"If you can find any other view of the world which agrees over the entire range where things have already been observed, but disagrees somewhere else, you have made a great discovery. —Richard Feynman, 1965"*

Another was a poster of one of her personal heroes: the celebrated mathematician and physicist Sophie Germain. *"It matters little who first arrives at an idea, rather what is significant is how far that idea can go."*

Professor Rutherford entered the room, awkwardly carrying an open briefcase. "I'll just be a few seconds more," he said as he set the case down, then fished around in the top drawer of the desk. She was mildly amused at all of the Post-It notes sticking out of the books in the professor's briefcase and watched as he scribbled "RT on Mon" on a new note and affixed it to the interior surface of the case. After a bit of rearrangement, he managed to close and latch the briefcase.

"There. Whew. Have a chair, please."

"I know that they probably wouldn't want you to say too much just now, but I've heard they're really onto something over there. Can you just confirm for me, please, just one thing that I've heard?"

Susan smiled and shrugged. "You probably know more about it than me."

"Well, I've been hearing about a rather remarkable ability to manipulate the Cherenkov field. You know about that, yes?"

"Yes, they've had something of a breakthrough in the accelerator's application as a quantum field generator, so that's opened up a whole new area where they felt they needed additional math expertise. And the ability to predict quantum interactions at certain phase values and frequencies has been an unexpected result. That's what everyone is most excited about, actually. I was there the other day and they were jumping around, really excited."

"So many people have been looking at that, but they actually got it working?"

"It sure looks that way."

Rutherford clicked his pen and scribbled a section of toroidal mesh on a pad of paper. "So, they shift through different phases *and* frequencies?"

"Yes, but dynamically. They're not static fields."

Rutherford smiled and dropped his pen. "Ah, that's something really no one anywhere has come close to, I think." He pressed his finger into the paper. "And of course, this is all something of a side effect of that accelerator running so fast. Yeah, that's really where all the interesting results tend to be. So, yes, they are really doing some of the best work in the world on quantum field effects. Maybe *the* best."

Susan nodded. "I agree."

"So, this, ah, device or method or whatever it is that

effectively cancels out the effects of Cherenkov radiation has allowed them to really push the envelope—almost in a literal sense—into some really leading-edge research... which I understand you are soon going to be a part of, yes?"

"They want math, they're gonna get some," Susan said with a smile.

He twirled the pen on the desk idly as he spoke. "Thanks for raising your hand. It sounds like a really exciting opportunity."

Susan grinned. "It sure is. I feel quite honored to have been invited to join their group."

"Yes. Um, to be honest, I recommended you. You've done very well here this year. They'll be lucky to have you."

"Thank you." Susan smiled graciously, pulling her backpack a little closer.

The professor opened the top drawer and retrieved a whiteboard eraser, then stood up and wiped off the whiteboard. *There's something else*, Susan guessed.

He paused, then turned back toward her. "I'm... *curious* as to what they've told you about the breakthrough."

There it was. "I really don't know if I'm allowed to say. I'm supposed to be signing an NDA today."

"Well, I'm sure they haven't told you everything yet, then," he said with a faint smile that dissolved as his brow furrowed. "It's really a new frontier and we really don't know exactly what's out there yet. Be careful, okay?"

Susan looked puzzled for a second, then smiled. "I sure will." She picked up her backpack. "I should be going. Thanks again for your recommendation."

As she turned to leave, Rutherford said, "Oh, one more thing. You didn't hear it from me, but Isaac Stern, the CEO of the org that owns MPAX, is fairly notorious for commercializing student-led innovations and then cutting them out of the profit picture. So, watch out for that, too."

"Good to know, thanks again," said Susan. "Bye Richard. You're a gem."

o o o

2

Math-Fu and the Cosmic Egg

Susan Everett felt slightly embarrassed about mispronouncing the name of the woman at the HR desk. Chichimecacihuatzin, the business card said. She had heard it twice at this point but she was still trying to work out the pronunciation in her head.

The woman pushed a form on a clipboard across the desk toward her.

"This is the NDA we will require you to sign. It's a fairly standard non-disclosure agreement, applicable to both verbal and written disclosures, in perpetuity. No interviews, no exceptions for the family, no tweets, no memoirs, nothing. Is that acceptable to you?"

Susan nodded.

"Please read it carefully and sign it in the areas highlighted in yellow." She pointed with the shiny and rather fake-looking rose-colored fingernail on her index finger. "There... and there."

"You are welcome to review it with a lawyer if you wish."

"That's not necessary. I've already consulted with a counselor, thank you. I'm ready to sign it now."

The woman handed Susan a blue pen. She signed the form in the indicated areas and handed the pen back to Ms. C.

"Thank you. We're excited to have you, and I'm sure you'd like to be briefed on the full scope of the project as soon as possible. I'll be right back with a copy of this for you. Would you like a cup of coffee or tea, or perhaps some water?"

"No, I'm fine, thanks." The way the woman said 'excited' seemed almost comical, she sounded so bored. Susan was very glad she wasn't an HR professional.

A moment later, the HR woman returned, holding a passcard on a black lanyard. She was accompanied by a balding middle-aged man in a white lab coat, and a younger, black-haired man in a blue sweater and black-framed glasses.

"Here's your temporary ID. Please look at the camera here and we'll get a photo for your picture ID. A little smile is fine. That's perfect, thank you. You can pick up your permanent ID badge here at this desk any time after noon tomorrow. Just give them back this temporary card when you pick it up, okay?"

"Sounds good, thanks."

"Susan, I'd like to introduce you to Dr. Erich Rössler... and Amir here is one of our wonderful interns. He's here for the summer, working on his practicum alongside Dr. Rössler's team. Gentlemen, this is Susan Everett, our newest hire. All the paperwork's done—she's all yours."

Dr. Rössler, looking slightly uncomfortable, slipped the smartphone he'd been holding into his lab coat pocket and extended his hand. "We're delighted to have you join us. Please call me Erich."

"Good morning, Erich," said Susan, briefly shaking his hand. She noticed that he seemed to be avoiding direct eye contact. His handshake was firm, though. She worried that perhaps hers had not come across as confident enough. She hadn't had a lot of practice at this.

A few seconds later, the intern stepped forward and extended his right hand. With the other hand, he pushed his glasses up his nose and swept his slightly unkempt hair aside. He looked young—probably no more than twenty.

"Amir. Amir Roy. It's a pleasure."

"Susan Everett. Pleased to meet you."

Amir shook her hand vigorously. "That's a good handshake you've got there, Amir," she said with a smile.

He beamed. "I really enjoyed reading your thesis on *Monstrous Moonshine*."

"Thank you," said Susan. "I'm still working on the infinite-dimensional graded representations for some of those conjectures, but yes, they are very interesting. Borcherds did some really terrific work on those."

"Definitely," said Amir.

"Amir will be available to show you around and help you find everything you need, said Dr. Rössler. "Let me show you to your workspace. That's right over here."

Dr. Rössler led Susan up a short flight of stairs to a small, windowless office on the mezzanine level. Amir followed close behind. Dr. Rössler gestured down the hallway. "My office is just down the hall, over there in the corner. You can usually find me there in the mornings or the late afternoons. However, Amir and I frequently spend most of the day down in the lab area with the engineering and science teams. I'll introduce you to them as soon as possible."

Dr. Rössler pointed toward the door. "Would you like a tour of the lab? You can see the HELX engine for yourself."

"It's really amazing," enthused Amir.

"It's operating now?"

"Oh yes. And it's working. Well, we *think* it's working. That's kind of where you come in. The mathematical interpretation of the, uh, superconformal symmetry is, uh, well, it's tricky, isn't it?"

"It sure is. Well, I'm looking forward to working on that with you and your team."

"I'll see if they're ready for us. Amir will accompany us to make sure you're well taken care of. And Amir will get you a lab coat, I think, yah?"

Amir beamed and nodded. Erich thumb-typed a message into his phone and tapped *send*. Then there was a moment of awkward silence.

After several seconds of nobody saying or doing anything, Susan spoke. "I want to tell you, Erich," said Susan. "I very much enjoyed your TED talk on The Unknown 95 last year. And I've just finished reading your piece on Conformal Field Theories. It's a very interesting paper."

This seemed to loosen the doctor up. He finally managed to look her in the eyes and a hint of a smile flashed briefly across his face. "Well, I'm delighted to hear that. In fact, that CFT work is exactly what we'd like to start you off with. We've got some—" Erich's phone suddenly buzzed. "Just a moment, please." He looked at it without raising it to his ear. "Ah, they're ready for us in the lab. It will make more sense once you see what we're working on down there. We'll just take that elevator...."

Erich pressed the smartcard at the end of the lanyard around his neck against the sensor on the elevator call-button panel. The touch panel lit up and displayed several available choices. He pressed L1. The cool blue LEDs switched from G to M2 and the gleaming doors slid open.

They entered the elevator and as the doors slid shut, Erich showed Susan the chip on his blue and white ID badge. "Remember to always swipe your card when you enter the building or the lab—and use the card to access the elevators. Keep it with you at all times, please. We'll get you fixed up with an email address and a computer later today. But first, let's meet the team, okay?"

o o o

Moments later, the elevator doors opened on level L1 and Susan, Amir, and Dr. Rössler entered the L1 lobby. "This is Lower Level 1, also known as L1," he explained.

Susan was surprised at how many people were working on this floor. Technicians bustled past the elevators and funneled into a large shared workspace behind a floor-to-ceiling glass wall. Others streamed into the corridors leading away from the opposite side of the lobby.

Erich pointed with his clipboard to the corridor on the left. "It's this way. Amir, please check with the Help Desk to see if they've finished applying the update. I'll take Susan over to CA1. We'll be back before lunchtime."

Erich read Susan's quizzical expression. "We're waiting for a firmware update. I'll take you over to see the Circular Accelerator."

Amir scurried off toward the other corridor and Erich held a door open for Susan. "It's this way. Oh—and never hold the door for someone like I just did. We're all supposed to use our own access cards. My bad."

The hall opened into a huge room, four stories high and at least two levels deep. Two levels down, a ramp led down to a large apparatus occupying the majority of the open space. Above them, elevators ran up the interior walls. Up on the top floor, a spectacular corner office was outfitted with curved glass panels and stainless-steel struts. That was probably Stern's office, thought Susan as she studied the steel-framed windows of the other inner surfaces of the building.

Looking down at the central chamber, Susan recognized some of the equipment. "It's a detector magnet system, yes?"

"It's actually a geomagnetic sync system that we use to stabilize the beamformers. There's another one way down at the other end of that corridor there. We use them to stabilize the coordinates of the quantum field. This whole thing started to pursue the same types of goals as they're chasing over at CERN, with the CMS and the ATLAS. You heard about the controversy over the safety of high-energy particle collision experiments? Well, we've been doing what some might call the dangerous stuff here, too. With some very interesting results."

Susan heard the faint clucking sound of her inner chicken. Not *too* dangerous, she hoped.

"Come this way. There's something else I want you to see."

"This hall leads down to an area known as the Annex," explained Rössler. "There should be a couple of electric vehicles down here." He led Susan around a corner, where a small shuttle vehicle was hooked up to an electric charger. "Ah, great, there's one charging. They won't mind. The system will show them where it is. Come on, this is kind of fun."

Erich and Susan got into the shuttle. "How do you steer this thing?" asked Susan, noting the lack of a steering wheel.

"It's autonomous," explained Erich. "It knows where to go." The subtle rising and falling of the pitch of the electric motor was soon drowned out by the sound of the rubber tires reverberating in the long hallway. As it carried them past glass-walled offices and conference rooms, Susan marveled at how remarkably long the hallway was. Finally, the shuttle slowed and turned toward a separate, newer-looking area of the complex.

"This is the main server farm here," said Erich, as the shuttle passed by a large glass-walled room full of equipment racks. "That's production, and that's staging over there. All the AI stuff runs on that big cluster."

"Pretty impressive."

As they traveled, Erich briefed Susan on her role and the problems they had encountered while compactifying the multidimensional fractal properties of the continuous-time dynamical system they were modeling. It was certainly not the kind of conversation in which Susan had the opportunity to engage very often. She felt very good about being here. And Erich was really lightening up.

She fantasized that she was in a *Geek Girl* comic strip, on an amusement park ride through a geek-heavenly tunnel of love, but with radioactive mutants. Ha.

"You know, we let the AI name this vehicle. You what it came up with? Autonymy 1! Means 'naming or designating itself.' Hah! Machine is trying to be funny, I think."

As their vehicle drove them down the long hallway, Erich was reminded of riding in a horse-drawn carriage, the first time his young wife and his younger self visited New York. Susan reminded him a little of his Marlena, so happy that day.

The vehicle slowed to a halt outside a section labeled CA1. Erich pointed to the ramp.

"Up there is that ramp we saw from above. This is the circular accelerator. It's just a platform so technicians can get underneath it from this floor, but there's another level beneath it, too. It's kind of like MPAX 2.0. We call it HELX, which stands for High Energy Large Accelerator. It's technically a wavefield synchrotron. It's like a combination of a superconducting synchrocyclotron and an isochronous cyclotron, but much more powerful than either one."

"Hmm," said Susan, trying to think of something polite to say. It looked rather unimpressive, compared to other circular colliders she'd read about.

"Don't be fooled by the small size. It's energy-equivalent

to a collider with a 100-kilometer circumference and a dynamic compensator for eliminating synchrotron radiation. Seriously. This thing rocks."

Erich pointed to a protruding cluster of what looked like wire-wrapped magnets.

"We're using a 256-Tesla high-field accelerator magnet array and a one-gigawatt radiofrequency acceleration system. And all that equipment along the sides, there, that's the cryogenics infrastructure. That's how we cool down the superconducting accelerator components. We think this thing could really crack the ol' cosmic egg."

He gestured with his hands as if manipulating an invisible Rubik's Cube. "We can tune this to very specific set of frequencies that dynamically rotate the magnetic field in sync with the particle acceleration. Simultaneous frequencies. And that's when things get interesting."

He pulled out his phone and apologized. "Pardon me, I have to check on that update." He tapped out a quick message and hit send. "There's a bug we're trying to find. We're just updating the firmware with what we hope will be the fix."

"Forget it," she said. "I'm used to it." This was nowhere near the worst case of cellphone distraction she'd had to sit through. Richard usually didn't even *think* to apologize at the worst possible moments.

Erich's phone buzzed. "Ah, great," he said. "The firmware update's all done. We should be good to go." He paused and rubbed his finger under his bottom lip for a moment.

"Hmm," he said, looking at a nearby print station, where a large-format laser printer was sitting idle. "On second thought, I'd like you to take a look at the math before we run any more tests. Do you think you could? We don't want to mess up again."

Erich quickly located the file on the department's intranet server and printed it to the nearby unit. A half-minute later, he handed the printout to Susan. "It's just a few pages," he explained. "Do you think you might be able to make sense of it?"

She riffled through the pages. It wasn't code—it was all formulae. "Not a problem. I'll look it over right now and let you know if I see any red flags."

"Oh, that would be perfect. We had some problems earlier last week and well, you know, I have to give a status report. So... no pressure, right?"

"Heh."

"So, let me introduce you to Karl Schraeder, our programming lead. He can explain the parts of the algorithm we've been fighting with."

He led Susan over to an engineer sitting at a nearby desk. In his hand he held a mug that said "If it ain't broke, it doesn't have enough features yet." As they approached, he put down the mug and sat up straighter.

"And this is Karl," said Erich.

"Karl, this is Susan. She's joining our team on the math side."

"Good morning," said Karl, in a fairly thick Austrian accent, as he rose to his feet. "It's still morning, ya?" He smiled at Susan and held out his right hand. "I am pleased to meet you."

Quite pleased, he thought.

Time to practice that handshake, Suzie...

Susan reached across the desk to shake his hand.

"That's a powerful handshake you've got there," he kidded. "If your math-fu is as strong as that, we'll be okay, huh? I'll make sure you are set up to use the bug tracker." Karl looked at his watch. "My apologies to you both. I have some things I must attend to. I beg your pardon, of course."

"See me this afternoon, Karl," Erich called after him.

"I will, Doc."

"He's like that," smiled Erich. "I'll brief him when he's got a few minutes."

Erich looked around for a moment, then said "Ah!" and pointed. "Over there by the elevator. See that woman with the black and blue hair? That is Li Yan, our engineering lead. I see she's on the move, so we'll have to catch up with her later. I think you'll like her. She's a very good engineer. Studied at MIT."

○ ○ ○

"Okay, everyone," said Erich, in his 'take charge' voice. "I've had a chance to brief Li Yan on the issues we'd like to run through in the tests with her engineering group, and she agrees that we should hold off on testing until we've implemented the fixes for the issues Susan and Karl found in our code review. Susan, you got that vector formula corrected pretty quickly—that was fantastic. Do you have a timeline yet for when you might be able to complete a review of the other sections?"

Susan pushed the mouse she was using away and stretched her fingers. "I'm pretty sure I can have all those formulas checked and corrected, if necessary, by the end of the day on Friday. Will that work for you, Karl?"

He made a note in his calendar. "Ya, that's good. And you can give me the data ranges we should expect to see. Okay?"

"Sure." She nodded and made a note of it.

"Li Yan, which sections will we be able to test in our Tuesday build?" asked Erich.

"Probably sections one and two for sure. Maybe section five."

"We can live with that, I think." Said Erich. No red flags.

"We should probably skip sections with the old formulas that Susan is ripping out," added Li Yan.

Susan saw Erich's eyebrows move ever so slightly. Explanation time.

"First of all, there are some geometries defined as lengths that really need to be changed to angles. Karl agrees that we should consider changing all the arrays in that section to vectors. It won't be faster, but it *will* be way more flexible for what we're doing. Karl wants to do it in multiple sprints, which is fine with me—I'm still getting up to speed with the AI routines Karl's team has implemented. They're using some pretty impressive heuristics."

"Yah, they're good," said Erich. Oh, by the way, if you hear us talking about Xavier, that's what we call the experimental algorithm's virtual reality front end. X-A-V-R."

"To be honest, we don't know what the hell that machine's doing some of the time, either," admitted Karl.

His Germanic sensibilities compelled him to explain further. "Li Yan and I added the new algorithms to the code library and we're now letting XAVR author and select the interpretive filters dynamically. It's a little hard to say for sure just yet, but it looks like the data interpretation routines are being successfully rewritten by the AI. If it passes the tests, we'll be able to run the analytics tools against the output to see which algorithms it is using."

"So, our job is evolving from programming the AI to understanding the output of the AI. The algorithm is self-documenting—supposedly—but it's outputting some very wild code."

"For sure," agreed Li Yan. "There's a section in there—it's the quantum expectation value of the stress tensor, specifically—that is frankly unlike anything I've ever seen. Multiple time vectors; really crazy stuff. I agree with Susan on that one—I really think we should skip those sections until we figure out what the AI is doing, but it will take some time."

Susan scrutinized the code on the screen for a moment before speaking. "Yeah, it's kind of a representation theory structure there, where the elements of a group referenced up at the top there are represented by invertible matrices; the group operation is handled like a matrix multiplication. It's like a Hilbert Space equation; sort of an infinite-dimensional vector space." She scratched her head, a little awestruck by the elegance of the math. "Pretty cool code, there, Karl."

"I wish I could get credit for that. But that's the machine's big idea. Maybe Li Yan, you know more about that?"

Li Yan stayed quiet long enough that Rössler took the hint.

"So, you think if we skip that section and whatever sections that depend upon it, you can deliver a status update next week that shows good progress?"

"Yep. Is that a decent plan, or would you rather wait until we've got all the routines validated?"

Karl, anticipating Rössler's next question, scrolled through the bug burn-rate stats.

"How long will that take?" And there it was.

"It's hard to predict exactly, of course," cautioned Karl, knowing that Rössler always demanded a more specific answer. "But, if we continue at the current burn rate, we should be able to have it ready by a week Thursday—at the earliest."

Rössler's eyebrows were always Karl's surest indicator of his mood. He knew Karl well enough to be confident that he wasn't inflating the estimate. But here, Karl sensed he needed more information.

"One of the things that's slowing us down a bit is the complexity here," conceded Karl. "Interpreting the documentation output from the AI is like reading the notebooks of a genius. It's a bit beyond all of us, I think—and I readily admit that I am directly responsible for the complexity of that output. I'll try and scale that back a bit in the next rev. But the debugger output looks solid. Every spot-test I'm doing of sections one, two, and five is coming back clean. We're going to throw the whole dataset at it next month, if we can squash enough bugs to get sections 3 and 4 to execute properly."

"Maybe it's best to do another review next Friday," suggested Susan, "to give us time to double-check those superpositions coefficients?"

Erich's eyebrows hinted at a frown. "I'll have to ask the board. They generally don't like us to release anything on Fridays, in case something goes south." He fidgeted with the phone in his hand. "And honestly, the reason the math team was decommissioned in the first place was the board's rationale for approving the whole AI program. We were only able to get you here due to a 'no compliance violation' provision in the service delivery contract that allowed for us to hire you as system support."

Susan closed her eyes. Never had eye-rolling felt like such an uncontrollable urge. "Well, I can shoot for EOD Thursday the 29th."

"Look," said Rössler, "I'm going to need to present this to the board at the end of the month. Amir, can you give me a simplified, executive-friendly PowerPoint on why we're testing, what we are fixing, when it will be ready, and why it's important? That's really the linchpin: what will happen if we run the new code on the previously approved firmware without further updates? Can you have a draft ready for my review by the end of the month?"

Amir wrote it down in his notebook and circled the 29th. "Yeah, I can do that."

Karl had been running through his part of the presentation in his head. "I strongly recommend not running through sections three and four. That firmware update still has some very funky code in those acceleration curves. I'm pretty sure there would be ringing artifacts, you know, false readings. I'll run the diagnostics for those two sections again and write an executive overview of those as v-next features."

One eyebrow went up. "Okay, okay, just put in very simple language for them."

"I'll send you an updated draft next Friday."

"Thanks."

○ ○ ○

3

Breakthrough

Amir was already in the room, fiddling with the presentation system's cables when the others entered.

"All right," said Erich, sitting down at the end of the table. "Let's run through the draft of your presentation. You be me giving the presentation, and I'll be the executives. I'll start the recording. Okay, let's go. Nice screen layout, by the way. Looking good."

Amir smiled as his thumb found the raised dot on the slide advance button. "If you see anything wrong, just let me know."

He began the slideshow and moved quickly past the department title screen. As he spoke, the presentation slides reinforced the key points.

"I'd like to begin by acknowledging that this is an interpretation of the work done by Li Yan's engineering group, and in particular, the AI team led by Karl Schraeder."

"As it *is* an interpretation of code developed in part by an artificial intelligence tool, the details are subject to change, as we learn more about the decisions that led to the present code-base, which for the record, is currently over 600 million lines of code. For context, a decent human programmer can write about 20 lines of code per hour. This code-base, therefore, represents more than 10,000 *years* of continuous human labor, assuming an 8-hour work day, no vacations, and only occasional potty breaks. And the AI built it just under 3 days. So, needless to say, there is a lot of code we haven't reviewed in detail. But the good news is, what we have tested appears to be nothing short of a major breakthrough."

"The next couple of slides are a summary of the key goals that were set several years ago for the AI routines themselves; I'm sure some of you have seen these slides before."

'And this one,' he imagined himself saying, 'is almost laughably oversimplified....'

"And now here we have a summary of the kind of systems we're seeing the AI build in the current codebase. I should also note that this code analysis is based on last week's build. We're still analyzing the changes made in the current build. But... long story short, the investments made on AI programming look like they are already paying off; we expect to see additional breakthroughs in the weeks and months ahead, dependent on continued investment in the development of the toolset, of course."

"Now onto some specifics: Interestingly, the program does not presume to know the type of data or the specific parameters it will encounter in its quantum simulations, nor does the resulting real-world output always match the observations made of the virtualized quantum realm. While that's not necessarily surprising, given the uncertainties of quantum mechanics, it does confirm the need for frequent testing."

"Change that to 'human' testing, okay? And get rid of that section that talks about the computer-assisted testing process. I don't want them to think that testing just magically happens."

Amir pointed to a footnote on the slide. "So, I should remove this bit about the CA1 test bed and the description of the virtualized environment running inside MPAS itself?"

Erich thought for a moment, then nodded. "Particularly important, I think, is to be clear that we deliberately removed the predefined dimensional limits built into our algorithm."

"Ah, okay," said Amir as he saved the edited text.

"Our story here is that we have rethought the way we are looking at the data. Previously, we would capture the data and then analyze it based on a standard four-dimensional matrix. The problem with those capture routines was that they made broad assumptions about what categories the data types should fall into. Special Relativity does not explicitly limit the number of space-time dimensions. So why should our routine arbitrarily categorize space-time dimensions as a four-dimensional Lorentzian manifold?"

Erich thought for a moment. "Too complicated for them! Just say 'four dimensions.'"

"Hypothetically, let's accept that there might be more than one 'time' dimension. If our metric tensor has a single negative eigenvalue that 'common sense' dictates should correspond to the existence of a 'time-like' direction, we would miss that secondary dimension, or at the very least, might misinterpret that data as something other than time. Or, if you prefer, what if there are five dimensions instead of four? Or ten. Who knows? Data collection and analyses need to be fully separated. And we should not presume that the data corresponds to our expectations. If anything, the quantum realm has already shown us the folly of that."

"Good, good points."

"This next part is Susan's section."

"So, Susan you're going to get up there and present this next part." Her cheeks involuntarily flushed a bit.

"And here to tell us more about the math behind this research, please welcome Data Scientist Susan Everett." As Amir, pretending to be a more gracious incarnation of Erich, extended his arm and welcomed her to the podium, the slide behind them changed to a diagram of a 3-D spiral.

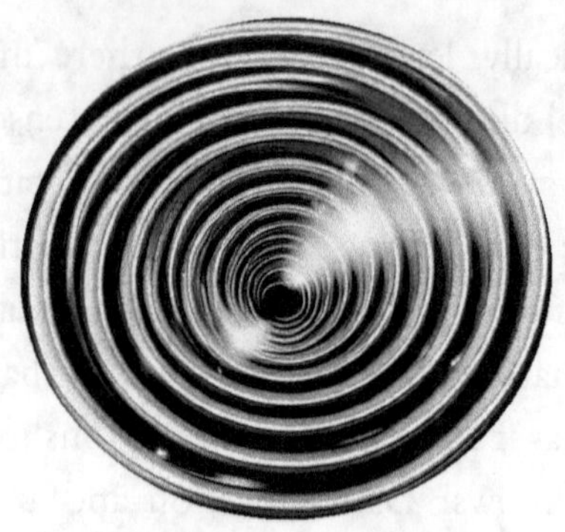

'Okay Suzie,' she thought to herself. 'Time to pretend like I know what the hell I'm talking about.'

"Albert Einstein believed time was a dimension 'like space.' And this got me thinking, you know, space is not one-dimensional. So why does almost every paper on General Relativity begin with something like 'assume a four-dimensional manifold M and a metric g'? You know, people always talk about the arrow of time, or the proverbial time line, so why does time suddenly get reduced to a single dimension as soon as we start talking about it in physics?"

"So, we thought," she continued, "what if time was a multidimensional construct, perhaps like a multidimensional spiral?"

"If this were the case," she went on to explain, "the passage of time could be measured by starting at the innermost edge of the spiral path and drawing an arrow straight toward the outer edge. We're assuming entropy increases as the spiral unwinds."

"Let's call this 'time's arrow.'"

"But what if you went forward along the path of the

spiral itself? You would still experience the passage of time, and you would still move forward through this dimensional path. But it's a different dimension than the one drawn by time's arrow."

"In other words, time does not travel in a one-dimensional fashion. Seeing time as an arrow moving 'forward' is, in effect, a one-dimensional way of looking at a multidimensional state."

"Now, to be clear, I am not suggesting that the essential nature of space-time is as simple as this diagram. I just want to illustrate a hypothetical example in which the passage of time is also subject to *lateral* movement, as it might be through causal multiverse transitions in the quantum universe."

Karl raised his index finger and caught Erich's eye. "It's worth mentioning that we did not specifically design the program executive to compute time in this sort of non-standard multidimensional way, but it was this thought experiment of Susan's that led us to consider the more interesting possibilities."

Susan smiled and changed slides to one with an overlay showing red arrows. "The way in which time's arrow resembles a straight line—or a pure quantum state, a ray in a Hilbert space—may be thought of as the path observed when one draws a line from the center of a disc—imagine the hole in an LP record—toward the edge of the disc."

"On this hypothetical disc, time travels forward as we approach the perimeter of the disc, and it also travels forward—albeit more slowly—along the path of the spiral. In this imperfect analogy, the still-probabilistic timeline ahead of the current position isn't recorded yet—it's more like a record-cutter than a 'backwards' record player. Nevertheless, time's arrow can be thought of as moving in more than one direction, although it is on a seemingly constant curve. As the disc rotates, grooves are cut into the record as three-dimensional waveforms, and as the recording progresses, the multi-state probabilism of the information changes and solidifies the recording into a single wave-state/quantum state. However, this wave-state may or may not be one dependent on wave-function collapse. It might instead be one that manifests as described in the Many Worlds interpretation."

The slide changed to a screenshot of the Wikipedia page describing the Many Worlds interpretation. Erich wrote the word Wikipedia on his notepad and then scratched a line through it.

Susan spoke again. "So, we started thinking, why not? Karl's code lets the system derive the dimensional structures based on kind of an elegance-seeking algorithm, based on the idea that we should not limit our assumptions about what the data will reveal by hard-coding wave function behaviors into the code-base, even if we think that common sense dictates that *of course* all quanta can also be described as a wave function, therefore *of course* the issue of 'distance' becomes irrelevant when examining the mysteries of 'spooky action at a distance.' *Of course* the answers to the mysteries are in fields and not in matter. Sometimes we expect waves but we see particles; sometimes we expect matter but we find energy."

Susan's next slide added a Z dimension to the spiral drawing. "All right. If we add more dimensions, then what?

The grooves on the disc begin to serve as an analogy for a multidimensional wave function operating as a field-wave, or something like that, let's suppose...."

She switched to a slide that animated the two dimensional-spiral rotating into a three-dimensional field.

"It's not hard to imagine the event-record's path as spiraling through multidimensional space. From any measurement point, we experience time's arrow and perceive a consistent flow-rate of time. Yet, when seen as a continuum, each one of those arrow-paths (probabilities) differs slightly—some more than others. And, like an analog recording, there is essentially no limit to the number of multiverse measurements we can make. They are all different—and the field is constant, continuous and analog—yet individual points in this multi-dimensional field may be measured as quanta."

Over the three-dimensional shape, the next slide again drew the 2-D spiral and marked an X at its leading edge.

"Okay. Continuing with our simplistic analogy, the event-record is being recorded, and the mechanism that cuts the grooves of the record operates at a predefined rate of movement, both forward and rotationally. We see and hear time moving forward. We see unwritten event-space (resembling uncollapsed wave function probabilities, but manifesting from MWI events) ahead of us, and recorded history behind us. And as the sphere (represented in simplistic form as a 2D platter, but in our case, the magnetic array) rotates, each section of the continuous spiral groove for each vector path also represents movement through time—albeit on a different scale. In other words, if we move laterally across that recorded surface, the 'playback point' also moves."

Erich nodded. "I think that's enough detail, provided that we make it clear that the predefined rate is relative and that we are treating time as a multidimensional entity. I guess we just won't dwell upon the whole wave collapse thing unless they specifically ask about that..."

"Not bloody likely," mumbled Karl.

Erich continued: "...and we lead them into the more technical discussions, but yeah, I can sell this."

"So that's all we have for our 'overview' presentation," said Susan. "But we also have a set of more technical breakout session slides, in case anyone wants more details. Do you want to see those?"

Erich looked at the clock and nodded. "Ya, but let's take a 10-minute break."

After the break, Li Yan continued with the more technical presentation.

"When viewed as an arrow from the current position of our hypothetical 'multi-D' record player's 'needle,' multiple starting points—in other words, multiple measurements— would show a different set of waves for each timeline, just as multiple straight lines drawn from the center of an LP record to the perimeter of the disc cross different wave-sections distributed around each track on the disc. In this view, time behaves as a scalar wave function, with longitudinal waves or 'tracks' propagating throughout the field and transverse waves like 'grooves', with 'crests' and 'troughs' recording the probabilistic multi-variances as they collapse into a single deterministic reality—per observer and measuring device."

Susan was trying her best to look interested. She found it hard to imagine that anyone they'd show this presentation to would appreciate its significance if they weren't a hardcore quantum mechanics geek. Fortunately, the room was full of them.

Li Yan continued: "In the model the AI has constructed, these longitudinal and transverse waves correspond to the open and closed strings of string theory, but with the strings being multidimensional (rather than one-dimensional, as in M-theory, or zero-dimensional, as with point-like particle physics). Notable differences from M-theory include the requirement for *two* time dimensions as per the Itzhak Bars theory of symmetry, plus physical dimensions as described in supersymmetric theory. 'Extra' dimensions are compactified due to their spherical/circular nature, and gravity and electromagnetism are unified as posited in Kaluza-Klein theory with the strong and weak nuclear forces as the fundamental forces of nature. It's all quite an interesting approach—different than anything we've considered before."

Susan glanced at Amir, who really did look interested.

"However," Li Yan continued, "Kaluza-Klein theory predicted a particle—which, in the AI's interpretation of wavefield theory, is a wave function instead. Similarly, Einstein's attempts at a UFT did not incorporate the strong and weak forces now generally accepted as features in the standard model. Fortunately, general relativity does not place any limits of the possible dimensions of space-time, and is fully compatible here."

The on-screen image changed to a diagram labeled 'Chirality' as Li Yan continued.

"Additionally, the eleven-dimensional supergravity model fails to account for the chirality inherent in the observed laws of physics—and enabled here by the 'two-time' dimensions of the AI's unique wavefield model and its multidimensional implementation of string theory—the five weakly interacting branes equivalent to the strongly interacting strings of higher-dimensional branes in ten-dimensional space-time."

"This," she explained, "corresponds exactly to type IIA superstring theory. It is also consistent with models that require the existence of objects with both electric and magnetic charge, as predicted by Montonen and Olive. So, it does seem plausible that it just might work."

The screen changed again, to show a conceptual model demonstrating a resonance effect.

"Overall, the conceptual model is similar to that of 'solitons,' where the fabric of reality is a product of mutual resonance of transverse waves of light and longitudinal gravitational waves.

The screen changed to show what looked like an onion-skin coming off in a spiral pattern.

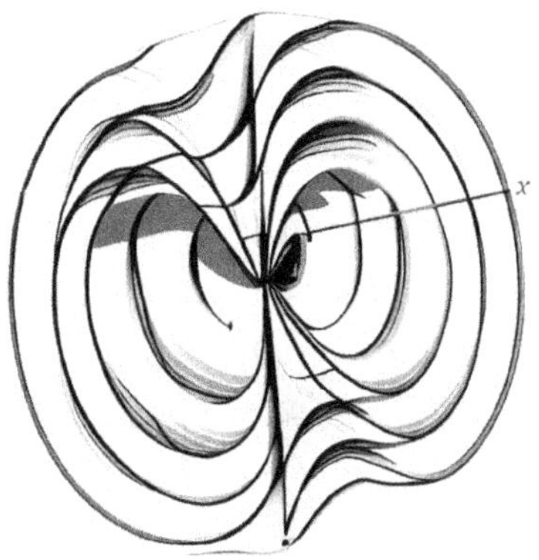

"As in the T-duality model, strings propagate around a spherical/circular extra dimension. A string has momentum as it propagates around the sphere/circle, and it can also wind around the circle one or more times, like a spiral onion skin— as per Witten, 1995."

She seemed to be wrapping up. Thank goodness, thought Susan.

"And, like the standard model, the AI-generated model allows a theory of gravity consistent with quantum effects. Thus, as per general relativity, the longitudinal waves are deformed by the curvature of space-time caused by the uneven distribution of mass/energy—in other words, gravity. In all, there's a lot more in the code to study, but it's looking like a remarkably robust model that our AI has constructed—and one we think is rich with potential for future research."

"Thank you, Li Yan," said Erich. "In summary, the model our team is developing helps to illustrate the idea that all particles can be fully described by wave functions."

He advanced to the next slide in the deck. It was captioned "extras and examples." He read it over.

Consider another example: the non-intuitive principle that looking at something changes it in the quantum realm requires a solution that avoids looking at it in a way that involves directly shining light on it (with various types of light being electromagnetic waves of differing frequencies).

Quanta and the notion of quantifiable particles, from this viewpoint, are irrelevant—they are all just wave functions. And, as postulated by Heisenberg, the paradoxical dualities inherent in quantum mechanics can be deduced as a specialized consequence of this field theory.

"Ahh, I think we can probably leave out those examples—and those Wikipedia bits, too. They are pretty challenging for an executive audience. So, we'll end it with the overview, and save the good stuff from Li Yan for the research crowd."

"And that's end of our breakout session." He stopped the recording.

"Bravo. Okay, allow a few minutes after each session for Q&A, and I think we're good. I'll schedule the meeting. Great job, everyone, thank you."

Susan's computer popped up a calendar notification for the executive meeting with Erich and the board. She unfolded the new lab coat sitting on the corner of her desk.

Moments later, Susan walked past the kitchen near the conference room. Li Yan was pouring a cup of coffee as Susan stopped to grab a bottle of water.

"I need this," said Li Yan with a smile. "Are you in this meeting, too?"

"Yep. See you in there," replied Susan.

"I'll be there in a moment."

"Okay, we're all here," said Erich. "Hi Susan, thanks for attending. Do you know George from Ops?"

The curly-haired man flashed a brief smile at Susan and acknowledged Li Yan as she entered the room and closed the door. He turned back toward Susan. "Dr. Rössler tells me you're our math whiz."

Susan smiled. "That's what we were all wishing for, I think," said George. "Welcome."

"Pleased to meet you."

"George," said Erich, "can you explain to us what's going on with the database?"

George turned to Li Yan. "Do you want to take this?"

"No, go ahead, George. Thanks for asking."

"Okay," George began, somewhat tentatively. "As some of you know, we have a continuous delivery model with our data warehouse. The pipeline to the field generators from the algorithm database is fed continuously, the production bits go through the pipeline anonymously and the database is non-transient by design. Over the past few years, we set up sort of an agile infrastructure so that schemas and content could be migrated around as needed or whatever. And that's fine—it's all working pretty well."

"The AI computes the field arrays and independently implements the models and structure that will take care of the data descriptions for the analytics systems, and sets up the operations it wishes to perform. And then it stores all of that in the database—pretty straightforward."

"We keep backups of the database, of course, and we test schema changes on a staging server, failing over to slave nodes and that sort of thing. Pretty standard stuff, until XAVR—that's the AI executive—dropped the latest set of libraries."

Li Yan nodded.

"As you probably know, XAVR has a summarizer module that parses the runtime output of a sandboxed version of the executable, so we have a summary of the changes, performance improvements and so on. In this case, however, the parser crashed entirely on a couple of the libraries. So, it took us a while to dig through the code and find the new routines. Very interesting new routines."

"It has constructed an entirely new way of connecting numerous microservices. It's no longer a single monolithic data store—and the AI has made a vast number of connections between the various cubes and data stores that, well, we just haven't seen the likes of before. It's very much in the style of our existing neural net, but dynamically rewriting itself as a continuous process."

"So, we put the runtime code on the staging server and let it run until it ran out of nodes. As you may know, we run the staging server with a much smaller number of nodes than the production environment."

"So, what we think we'd like to do now is let it loose with a full set of nodes. We'll let it make those new connections and then run the analyses. That's really what we're asking management to approve at this point."

"And DevOps is fully behind this?"

"Yes, absolutely. We estimate six hours of downtime at

most for the configuration change, and then another six hours to restore operations if we need to roll back."

Erich nodded approvingly. "I'll take it upstairs to Stern right away. If we get the approval, when do you want to go ahead with this?"

"Well, management likes Thursdays. Either that or it's overtime for ops on 'Patch Tuesday.'"

"Yeah. I'll ask for Thursday."

o o o

Thursday

Susan's phone buzzed. It was a text message from Dr. Rössler.

Something unexpected has happened. Meeting w Karl at 17:00 in conference room M102. Can U attend?

Another late dinner, thought Susan.

A few seconds later another text appeared.

URGENT

When Susan arrived at the meeting, Erich, Karl, Li Yan, and a bald-headed man she didn't recognize were already there. Li Yan was idly stirring her coffee as Karl fiddled with a laser pointer.

As Susan sat down, Erich said, "Okay, let's get started. There's a lot to cover and I've got a hard stop at 5:30 p.m." He turned on the projector in the conference room and flipped past a title screen to an image of waveform data. "Karl gave me a very brief summary of the situation, and I thought we should review this together, so I called this meeting. Karl?"

Karl used the laser pointer to highlight a spike in the complex waveform on the screen.

"Hi everyone. As you may recall, we just ran the new routines on the full dataset and, well, something unexpected has happened. He pointed to the leading edge of the spike on the screen. Here, at 15:05 today, *this* happened about five minutes after the new routines went live on the production cluster."

"Actually," said Li Yan, "It was almost exactly 30 seconds after we started the first run on the accelerator." With her eyes, she attempted to lead Erich's attention toward the bald-headed man. It wasn't working. "Pardon me, Erich," she said. "Who is our guest today?"

Erich glanced at the bald-headed man and cleared his throat. "Oh, my goodness. I was so wrapped up in all of this I forgot to introduce this fine gentleman here. This," said Erich with his arm outstretched, "is Dr. Eldon Johnson, a cosmologist from the Physics department at the university. I pulled him in here as a subject matter expert on what I think we may be seeing here. Dr. Johnson, can you share your thoughts on what might be going on here?"

"Thank you, Dr. Rössler. Hello everyone. Yes, this is something exciting we are seeing here—and of course very unusual. Perhaps I may ask if any of you know what the Alcubierre metric is?"

"Ah," said Li Yan. "Is it related to that warp drive idea?"

"Very good. Yes, it is. We think we might be seeing something like that here. Some sort of hypersurface, like a warp ring—complete with a time dilation effect."

"Really? Well, that *is* interesting. I thought that idea required exotic matter."

"Well, so did we," said the professor. "But it looks like it's a conformal gravity effect."

"Hm. Bizarre. So, how is it manifesting?"

"Well, as far as we can tell from your data—and thank-you to Karl here for that—the effect conforms to the Einstein field equations, but running in the other direction. But look here—it seems like the weak energy condition is not being violated. So, no exotic matter required?"

"Hmm. Very weird indeed. So, what, time travel?"

"Maybe," said the professor. "It looks like you might be able to jump forward, at least."

"Oh good," mused Karl. "I'll get caught up at last. Oh wait, I'll be further behind."

"So, what are the next steps?"

"We mostly need to figure out exactly what is happening here and make sure we haven't created a dangerous situation here already. Before we do any more testing, we really need to think about these two things."

Susan pointed to the screen. "Okay, can you run through this sequence for me? Exactly what was going on when it spiked?"

"Well, just before the spike, we had the beam-forming routine running and we were oscillating the warp ring."

"And there's the contraction. See? The time's wrong."

"17 seconds! Well, closer to 17 and a quarter. I'll see if I can get an exact number for that."

"Hmm."

"Wait," said Li Yan. "If something shifts suddenly in time

while the earth is spinning and the galaxy is rotating, and the universe is expanding, how would that even work?"

Karl thought about it for a moment. "I would imagine that it would mean that our geomagnetic sync signal was doing what it was designed to do."

Li Yan nodded. "We map the time-space coordinates based on the sync signal, so in principle, it *should* work anywhere."

"So, could we place a receiver that can pick up signals from an identically tuned receiver?"

"No way. It's never going to be identically tuned."

"But if the wave propagates forward, we should be able to sync to it."

"So, we can send things forward, from as far back as the wave has existed."

"Hm. Not especially useful, but interesting."

"The math predicts that there should be a ring of light," said Eldon. "I've already verified this with Professor Rutherford at the university."

"Yes, yes," said Dr. Rössler. "That's why we pulled you in here, Eldon. We're pretty sure that what we're seeing here is the real deal."

"Can we get a high-speed camera to monitor the field effects? The theory is that we should see fringing during the collapse phase."

"We've only sent sound and light and some analog representations of data, given the wavefield's characteristics. We have not even tried to send anything physical."

"Well, that would be worth trying. I'll work on the risk evaluations for that."

Rössler handed him a card. "It might be useful if you could work with Susan on developing this displacement model a bit, yes?" Susan wrote down her email address on the back of the card for him.

"But if we'd already broken the universe, we'd probably know it by now, right?"

"I hope so."

4

Regression/ Progression

The next day, 4 p.m.

Li Yan hung up the phone. "Hm," she mumbled and scratched her head. "That was George," she said to Karl and Susan. "He says the latest revision of the AI executive has rewritten that entire Chirality section of the system software."

Karl fumed. "What the—? We hadn't even finished analyzing it."

Susan wanted to ask who in the *hell* thought it was a good idea to even allow a system software update at this juncture, but thought it might be better not to go there. It was obviously George.

"Well, it appears that the code was incompatible with some other objective. It's ironic that XAVR has created this situation by choosing to deprecate outcomes that are outside the scope of its programmatic objectives."

Erich rushed down the corridor. He'd obviously just heard the same story. "Tell me we have a backup?"

"Yes," said Karl, "but the pre-regression codebase has known conflicts with the libraries used on the current firmware version."

Susan thought she heard Erich swear under his breath. "So, we have to roll back the firmware, too?"

"That is not trivial. We will miss *all* of our deadlines if we do that," Li Yan warned.

"I don't care," said Erich. "Make it happen. How soon can we be ready to restart from the backup?"

Karl scratched out some estimates on a notepad. "Mm, it's about two terabytes of system code, not including several petabytes of training data, which is all stored separately. That takes a bit less than six hours to restore, and then a couple of hours for Li Yan's team to reflash and verify the firmware. Then, another five or six hours for George's team to cover all the physical systems checkpoints. So, maybe by end of day tomorrow? Not including startup time. Ya, 14 hours to operational status, I'd say. I'll have to make sure George's team is fully available."

"That throws us off schedule by roughly two working days," noted Li Yan.

She was shocked when Erich scarcely blinked. "Okay, good. Do it." He *never* did that.

"What about the board?" she asked. Surely, he would have to trot this upstairs for Stern's approval.

"I'll take responsibility. Get George down here and anyone else we need and tell them we'll set up camp in room L101, ringside. And find Amir. Tell him to keep notes and start up a project doc with the task list, okay?"

And without waiting to hear the answer, he rushed off again.

"I would *not* want to be George today," whispered Li Yan to Susan.

Susan flashed a terse smile. "As Grace Hopper once said, 'it's easier to ask forgiveness than it is to get permission.'"

"She said that? I thought it was an old saying attributed to one of the queens of England."

"Well, maybe it was. Whatever. I read it in a book about Hopper, who was a pretty cool lady."

"I doubt George will get much in the way of forgiveness, unfortunately," said Li Yan. "I've seen Rössler mad before, but never like *that*."

○ ○ ○

"Ringside" was the informal name for the ring of workspaces extending from the offices on the east side of the accelerator to the cubicles at the other end of the control room's semi-circular wall. Room L101 was the name of the largest conference room in that area. Unlike the other offices and smaller meeting areas, it had glass panels on both the inner and outer exterior walls and six large monitors mounted on the wall farthest from the door.

"We need a whiteboard in here." Erich pointed his finger impatiently. "Amir."

Amir looked up over his laptop screen. "Um, I could project the tablet output to a screen if that would be better."

"No, I *want* a whiteboard, thank you."

Susan felt the tension in the room. "Would anybody like a coffee or a soda or something?"

"That's a good idea. Amir…"

Amir had already left.

Erich exhaled heavily and put a hand flat on the table next to Karl's laptop. "Sure, Susan, that would be nice. A few bottles of water and some juice, if you don't mind. Great."

Seconds later, Amir opened the glass door and wheeled in a whiteboard. "I still have to get some more dry-erase markers. But these two should get us started."

Erich eyed the red and black markers. "Yeah, a green and a blue would be good. That's great, right over there, thanks. Susan's just getting us some sodas. Anything else we need? Pens? Pencils?"

Amir clattered down a collection of writing implements. "Nah, we're pretty much set for pens and pencils."

"Great. Okay." Erich's phone was buzzing.

"Ah, it's George." He glanced at the clock on the wall.

"Yes, Ringside on L1. See you there. Yes, Li Yan's on her way. Thank you."

By mid-afternoon the next day, Erich's end of the conference room table was cluttered with coffee cups and empty juice boxes. Amir was busy transcribing whiteboard notes and Li Yan and Karl were looking at code on Karl's laptop. On the far side of the table, Susan was punching numbers into Mathematica on her own machine.

About a minute before 3 p.m., she smiled and looked up. "Aha," she said. "I received a set of equations last night from Dr. Johnson and plugged them into my simulation. And I think we have something here. The professor thought we may have experienced what is known as a ringfield effect. It's part of the Alcubierre metric equation.... Sort of a toroidal bubble. And sure enough, the numbers are checking out. The effect we saw should be reproducible."

George's phone buzzed almost precisely at 4 p.m. "We are ready to rock," reported George. "The system is ready anytime we are." He checked the dashboard display on his screen. "Monitoring is up, field integrity is good."

Erich flashed a weary smile. "Great. Okay, let's see it up on the big screen."

Susan was impressed with how well Erich was managing his anger to toward George. Rather than undermine the group with negativity, he was being downright supportive—and the benefit to the group dynamic was obvious. This was an insight into his management style she'd never had before.

As the accelerator field strength status indicator reached one hundred percent, ripples suddenly appeared on the surface of the water in Susan's bottle. "Oh, look!" she said excitedly, pointing to the water. "Did you feel a vibration?" she asked the others.

Karl shook his head.

Li Yan pressed her hand on the large pane of glass next to the door. "Hm, little or no vibration here."

"I didn't feel it," said Amir.

"Me neither," shrugged George.

"Easy to check," said Karl. "Nope, nothing showing in the latest seismic network data."

"A big truck, maybe?" suggested Li Yan. Amir peered into Susan's water bottle.

Erich was standing near the door by the whiteboard. He uncapped the red marker and wrote 4:01 p.m. Ripples/Vibration. "Well, we'd better shut it down and run a diagnostic to see if everything's okay," he said. "Karl?"

"I'm on it." The electrical hum of the magnetron faded as Karl spoke.

Erich swung open the door and looked up and down the hall. "That's odd. It's weirdly quiet out here."

Li and Karl looked at each other, puzzled. Karl said, "Ya, 4 p.m. There should be people in the halls, for sure. Or at least the coffee room. The kitchen, I mean, you know."

"I've got to go to the washroom anyway. I'll drop by the security desk."

A few minutes later Erich returned, with his phone in his hand. "This is weird. All of the clocks in the other areas are off by roughly 23 minutes. I took a video—see? —and the clocks are still running. And there's nobody here. And there's tape across the door."

Amir shook his head. "Wait, what...?"

Typing quickly, Karl opened a command shell on his computer. A few seconds later, the video from a remote webcam displayed on his screen. "I don't think it's been 23 minutes. It's *dark* outside." He typed furiously. A series of network diagnostics appeared in the command shell. His eyes narrowed. "What is this?"

Karl's eyebrows furrowed as he studied the diagnostics data. "Look at this. This is... runtime output here and that is the log output there." He directed Erich's attention to his screen. "The server thinks it's 4:25. So..." He scrolled up through the data. So, where is 1600 in *here*?"

"Check your phone," suggested Li.

Erich was visibly distressed. "I'm going upstairs." He looked down at his phone and frowned. "Just a minute. I can't seem to reach anyone."

"Hmm. Me neither. I'll come with you," said Amir, grabbing a notepad.

Susan and Li peered over Karl's shoulders as he typed.

"I'll put this up the big screen," he said as his fingers flew across the keys. "Just a sec. Okay."

A faint ring of light appeared momentarily on the high-speed recording.

"See? Look at that. It's not 4:25 p.m.—it's 4:25 in the morning. *Tomorrow* morning."

○ ○ ○

The elevator door opened on the main floor and Amir poked his head tentatively through the open door. "It's quiet."

"Come on. Let's go to the security...."

Just then, a security guard came around the corner. He held his fingers over his right ear and spoke into his microphone. "Two men. Hold on, it's Rössler."

The guard rushed over, eyeing Amir's orange security badge. He turned his attention to Erich. "Are you okay, sir?"

"Yes, yes, we're fine. What's going on?"

"Well, we locked the place down when you went missing. Do you know the whereabouts of the others?"

"You mean Karl Schraeder, Li Yan Zhang and George... ah, Gunderson. George Gunderson?"

"And Susan," offered Amir.

"Ah yes, of course, Susan Everett. Yes, yes. Everyone's fine."

The guard spoke into his mic. "All accounted for." He looked at his watch. 4:28 a.m. "Cancel the alert, will you?"

"Roger that," said the voice over the radio.

The guard extended a hand toward the security desk area. "Doctor, would you and Mister Roy here mind coming with me to the desk? We have some questions," said the guard.

"So do we," said Erich.

o o o

The two of them stood at the Security Desk counter as the guard picked up a clipboard and pen and conferred quietly with a seated guard stationed behind it, in front of a bank of video monitors. He ran his finger down the page, then put a checkmark next to E Rössler. He then walked over to Amir. "And you are...?"

"Amir Roy." He turned his head and noted a misspelling on the form. "With an A."

"Where are the others on your team, Dr. Rössler?"

Erich gestured with the palm of his right hand in frustration. "We've been in L1, the big room on the lower level. Working, you know?"

"The whole time?"

"Yes, the whole time," said Erich, as annoyance crept into his voice.

The guard looked puzzled. "Really? Hmm. L1. Okay." He wrote down L1, then pressed the mic button and spoke. "We're, uh, heading down to L1 now. I'll confirm the others *asap*. Over."

When the elevator door opened on the lower level, they saw Susan standing outside the door of L1, her arms folded in front of her.

"Everything okay?" asked Erich.

"Well, we were starting to wonder," said Susan, tensely.

The guard noted Susan's badge and placed a check next to her name on his form.

"Let's go inside," said Erich, gesturing with his head. "Everything's fine."

"Well, it's not fine," protested Susan. Erich raised his fingers to quiet her. "We'll do a full investigation. I promise."

Susan exhaled heavily and looked over to meet Li Yan's eyes, silently acknowledging her concern as the guard checked off ZhangL and SchraederK on his list.

The guard looked suspiciously at George. "Where's your badge?"

"Oh, haha, sorry. Here." George stood up and wiggled the badge clipped to his belt.

The guard spoke into his mic. "419. Yeah, all accounted for. Okay, cancel the alert."

"Roger."

"Okay," said the guard, flipping to the second page of

notes on his clipboard. "So... where were you at, uh... about 21:00, last night?"

"We were here. Right here. Yeah, definitely."

"Did you go out for dinner or leave the room?"

"Did you remove your badges for any reason?"

Erich looked annoyed. "No. Not at all."

"Hmm," murmured the guard as he scratched the side of his head with his pen and wrote a question mark in the column labeled "reason."

The desk phone at the security desk buzzed. The other guard picked it up. "CA1, Kevin here. Yes sir. I'll tell him, sir."

The second guard leaned close to Erich's ear and spoke quietly. "May I speak with you in private, Doctor?"

"Of course. Kevin, is it?" The guard nodded.

"One moment, please, Amir."

Amir stepped back, feeling a little awkward.

The guard directed Erich's attention to the second of six video screens at the desk. "We have a video capture from the security cam on L1 we'd like to review with you. It will just take a moment, if you don't mind."

"Certainly, certainly."

"Okay, bring up L1 for review."

"And there is 03:00. No one there. Okay, let's skip forward a bit. There's 4:00. Still nothing. And look, here's 4:23:01. And there you are. And that's Will on night patrol, down the hall there."

"Can you go back just a few seconds to 4:22:48 am? Just a few seconds before the 48-second mark..."

"Sure, yeah."

"Ah, there!" The video showed papers rustling in a trash-can outside one of the office doors just down the hall from L1. Stepping through the video, it was apparent that a new piece of garbage suddenly appeared in the can, disturbing the other trash. And there again on the high-speed recorder was a faintly glowing ring.

"Interesting."

"Can we also go back to the day before yesterday, at 15:00? Oh, but a different area – Main Control on L1."

"Sure, it's a different file, but yeah, no problem." He wrote MCL1 in the margin of the paper on the clipboard.

As Amir examined the leaves on one of the small trees in the lobby in between frequent glances at the desk, Erich and the guards spent several minutes reviewing the video from 15:05:00 through 15:05:16. The field of view in the video showed just an empty chair. Kevin the guard set the playback time to 15:05:17. "Ah, there you are," he said. At 15:05:17 on the video time indicator, someone had appeared at the Control console. "Mm, that's not me," said Erich.

Kevin the guard put down the clipboard next to Will. "So, where were you?"

Erich eyed the guard over the top of his glasses. "That's a very good question."

o o o

5

An Essential Ingredient

"Okay, let's head back, Amir," said Dr. Rössler.

"I could see you watching," said Erich with a wry smile as he swiped his card underneath the elevator command panel and pressed L1 when it appeared on the touchscreen. "You might have been listening too, yeah?"

Amir looked a little sheepish. "Well...." As they waited at the elevator, Amir asked, "What's going on with the video?"

The elevator doors slid open and they stepped inside. Amir had always thought these elevators were inconvenient, with their complete lack of buttons on the inside of the elevator. But today, it was apparent to him that this was all part of the security system. No one gets to come down here without explicit permission.

"I have an idea," said Erich, "but wow, this is really something amazing. It's something really big." Suddenly, Amir realized this wasn't just a security exercise or an electrical system foul-up. He hadn't seen Erich this enthusiastic about, well, *anything.*

Amir's stomach growled. "You're really hungry, I think?" said Erich. "Ya, me, too."

The elevator door opened into the glare of the L1 lobby lights. As they neared the conference room, Erich noted the time on his phone. Through the unfrosted half of the window near the door, Amir could see Susan and Li conversing as they stood behind Karl, who was typing furiously. Li was nodding in apparent agreement with something Susan had said.

"And Professor Rutherford said he thought…"

She paused.

Erich held the door open and Susan entered the room, followed by Amir. Erich stayed outside, quietly speaking to someone on his phone—probably his wife—as the door slowly closed.

"My apologies for being away for so long."

A moment later, he entered the room. "Hey guys," he said. "Let's go have breakfast, or lunch, or whatever meal time it is —my treat." The mood in the room improved immediately.

"We'll keep the room. Don't worry. I have it reserved until noon tomorrow. Your stuff will be safe. We'll leave the lab coats here and go, you know, *incognito.*"

"How about the food court over at the mini-mall?"

"Sure."

"Great."

"Fine."

"Yah, okay."

They decided on Chicago-style Gourmet Hot Dogs. Li Yan had a Tofu Veggie Dog.

"Karl went very deluxe here, I see," said Erich with a smile, noting the pile of toppings smothering the frankfurter on his plate.

"It's 'The Works,'" explained Karl, licking his lips playfully. "They call it the Whistler."

"Heh, sounds like Vancouver, not Chicago," said Susan.

Amir obviously recognized the name. "Uh, I think it's the Dog Whistler," said Amir, tentatively.

"The full name is The Dog Whistler," confirmed George. "And Whistler is closer to Squamish, not Vancouver."

"I don't think 'Dog Whistler' means what you think it means," laughed Susan. "It's really a very unsavory name for a food product."

"But people *do* call it 'The Whistler,'" Karl playfully protested. "I call it 'very tasty.'"

"If you like sauerkraut, that is," he added, taking a big bite.

"It's such a weird name for a hot dog," marveled Li Yan. "Règǒu. But there used to also be Whistle Dogs, a different type of hot dog, right?"

Erich nodded. "I remember those, yes," he said, wiping the corners of his mouth. "I had a job at the place they made those once upon a time. When I was a teenager."

George giggled, covering his mouth with a paper napkin. "Our Erich?"

"What?"

"Nothing, sorry," said George, imagining a teenaged Erich

with a stupid hat, flogging fast-food hot dogs from behind a food court counter somewhere.

"Yes, even I was a teenager once. Hard to believe, I know." He gestured with his half-eaten Chicago Dog. "They were not like this, though. These are really good."

George was looking at a list of search results on his unusually large phone. "It says here they discontinued Whistle Dogs back in 2016. Bummer."

"God you're old, Erich," teased Li Yan.

"Yah, all the better for these Chicago Dog guys, I guess," said Karl, finishing off his meal.

"Okay, everybody…" Erich said in his leadership voice. "As much as I know you'd all like to come back to the office and help me figure out what the *hell's* going on over there, it's been an awfully long day. Let's call it a day and meet tomorrow morning at 9 a.m. sharp, okay?"

There was a collective sigh of relief. Erich smiled and rubbed his chin. "Wow, I need a shave."

o o o

At 9:01 a.m., Erich explained that his dog had been much happier to see him than his wife. He apologized and thanked everyone, aware that the people on his team were in a difficult position, bound as they were by non-disclosure agreements.

Karl didn't say anything, but Mrs. Schraeder had been *very* skeptical when he told her they had been at the office all that time. This was not the first time he hadn't come home.

"Let me begin, okay?" asked Erich. He opened up his laptop, and mirrored the display on the room's big screen before continuing. It was a Mathematica model of the toroidal field that Susan had sent him. "I think Susan might be onto something here, with this toroidal ring-thing." He traced a crude oval around the model in bright red. "The ringfield, yes. Maybe four dimensional. Maybe more."

"I predict we will find more than four," said Karl. "This firmware is set up to allow for more."

"Any ideas... or thoughts?"

Susan acknowledged him with a polite smile and spoke more deliberately. "Let's review the data."

"Susan, go ahead, you take this part," said Erich. "I'm so busy thinking about this. It's—ah...." He shook his head. "It's amazing. I think we've really got something here."

Susan connected her laptop to the big screen. On it appeared a geometric model of a slightly flattened toroid with a mesh overlay that looked like a spiral with a hyperbolic warp. Susan zoomed the window to fill the whole screen. "Ok, so here is the accelerator—circular shape there. We're here." Susan gestured with her hand as she spoke. "Here's what we know:

15:05 three days ago, we lose—or *gain* depending on your point of view—roughly 17.25 seconds. There's a perturbative effect—a glowing fringe for a few seconds—probably too faint to see with the naked eye unless it's very dark. We see a spike. Lots of data for 17.25 seconds, then boom. The spike ends, we lose that time."

"We jumped *past* it, so it's lost," opined George, rather pointlessly.

Susan continued. "Then at 4:00 p.m. the next day, a bigger

jump, to 4:23 a.m. yesterday morning or thereabouts—with the old firmware." She underlined the words old firmware.

"And we had to regress the software," Li Yan reminded her. "Right, of course. Yes, thanks. Old software."

"We run the old code on the old firmware and it works even better, and we jump about 12.38 hours forward. But the data looks normal. No spikes. And I saw ripples in the water. I thought it was an earthquake."

"Or a big truck," added George, leaning back in his chair.

Li Yan sighed audibly.

Erich had his finger up. "And," he added, "the security cam video showed a change. A sudden change in the garbage can. I've got the clip cut out here."

"Oh?" said Susan, "Let's see that. We'd all like to see it, I'm sure."

Karl and Li Yan nodded. "Definitely," said George.

"I'll do that," offered Amir, doubling as tech support. He put down his pen and switched video cables. "We should just do the video wirelessly."

"This is fine," said Susan. "Thanks."

"So, what will we be seeing here, doctor?" she asked.

"Just hit *Play*. It's a short clip. It plays just the transition part here. Watch closely. There. Like there was a piece of video footage cut out or something. Almost exactly 4:22:48."

Erich set it to loop. "There, look at that. That could create a little wind."

"No fringe, though," noted Li Yan.

"The math predicts that it's there. Just too brief or faint to see with the unaided eye."

"There were reports of wind in the hall. That's what the guards said." He selected a different video and tapped *Play*. "But the big thing," noted Erich, "was this video. Look, this is our room. This room. But it's empty. The wrong room. And here, at 4:23, it's the wrong people, wrong time, something's puzzling. And amazing of course."

Susan was thinking out loud. "Somewhere along the line, our universe is different. And the new software doesn't run at all on the old firmware."

"It could be fixed," said Karl, studying the runtime log. "Given enough time, of course. Haha." Suddenly, he inhaled sharply. "Oh, *this* is interesting," he said. "The firmware update process ran again. It updated itself in that 12.2-hour period after that run, before we took the system offline."

"Well that's inconvenient," said George.

"Terrible, you mean," said Karl.

"Different how?" asked Li Yan.

"I have no idea," admitted Karl. "But I'm taking the version controller offline, so this doesn't happen again." He mumbled to himself. "Damn, I should have done that earlier."

Amir made a note of the runtime log timestamp and circled it on the whiteboard.

Erich sighed. "We'll test this new firmware separately. First, we have to get through the version that produced the anomaly. Susan, please continue."

Karl looked up. "Oh, sorry, I interrupted you. Oops." It was hard to tell if he was being sarcastic.

Erich studied the runtime log intently, thinking out loud. "Remember, the new software doesn't have this unusual code.

The last software compilation rewrote that entire section. It removed the whole conformal field section. The program's solution to some other core objective messed it up..."

"And we have to work overtime to fix its screw-up," said George.

Li Yan rolled her eyes.

"I think we don't need the new software. The old software/firmware combo is pretty good. Maybe we would tweak that. It's close, though. And the effect—it's reproducible."

Susan thought. "What else?"

"Well my beard grew normally, noted Erich. "So, my body clock didn't go through a sudden transition. That's good, I guess. I'm younger."

"You can sell that," said Li Yan.

"I think a logical step would be to set up a diagnostic analysis to look for something that would allow variable times. She circled the 17 on the screen. "17.25 seconds, then later 12.38 hours. Same software, bigger jump. Both running on the old firmware.

But it's not clear why we get different results from two runs that—it seems—should be similar. But they're not very close."

"The obvious next step would be to run the accelerator for exact periods of time and see if there's a correlation with the power stepping values. If you see that ripple effect," he said, "be sure to report it."

George nodded. "There's bound to be *some* relationship."

"There could be some danger though," cautioned Erich.

"I think we should start with small values." Susan smirked and held up a drawing in her notebook.

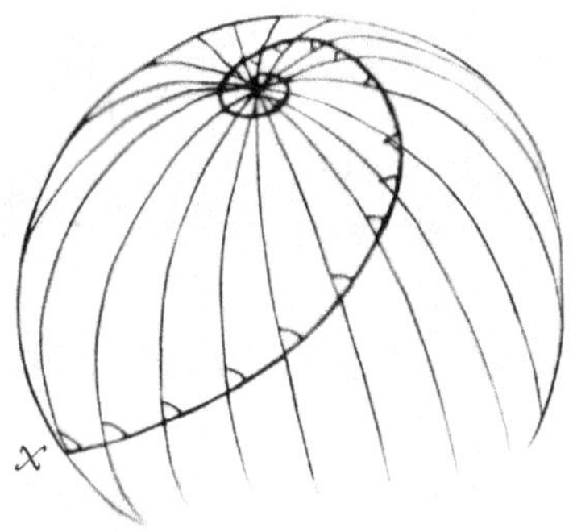

*Based on a drawing by Jean Pierre
Petit*

"The displacement value this program is using is based on a Fibonacci sequence. This is because the meridians of our bubble field are its geodesics—and any path crossing the meridians at a constant angle other than 90 degrees invariably winds toward one of the poles in a Fibonacci-like spiral. It's like nature's model is 'You can't go wrong with a Fibonacci.' No, I'm kidding. The doctor is correct, of course. We need to be very careful and methodical about this. Proper documentation is very important here."

Amir looked up, feeling the burden of responsibility.

"Not just Amir, that means everybody," said Erich. "We have to do a good job here. And don't discuss this with anyone. Absolutely no one. I'm not kidding. This is important." The others nodded in acknowledgement.

He thought for a moment. "You know, it's a good idea, Susan. When XAVR removed that Z-Helix library, the whole thing broke. We put it back in and fixed it. It might be innately connected. It adds the ingredient of Nature's elegance."

"So we know the firmware is a factor," added Amir, with a hint of uncertainty in his voice.

"And that was thought to be broken by the AI the first time we replaced it," noted Karl.

Li Yan uncapped a dry-erase marker. "I remember when we were planning the multidimensional data capture routines for the system, and we thought it would actually be a really good test sequence to determine Z-dimensional representations."

"Ya, that paid off big time, hey?" recalled Karl.

Li Yan nodded. "It certainly proved worthwhile in terms of allowing us to compare and isolate effects based on run-time and real time. We would get a zero value, two single-unit values to make sure we get two nearly identical results, a multiple of that, and other good stuff."

She drew a spring-like shape on the whiteboard.

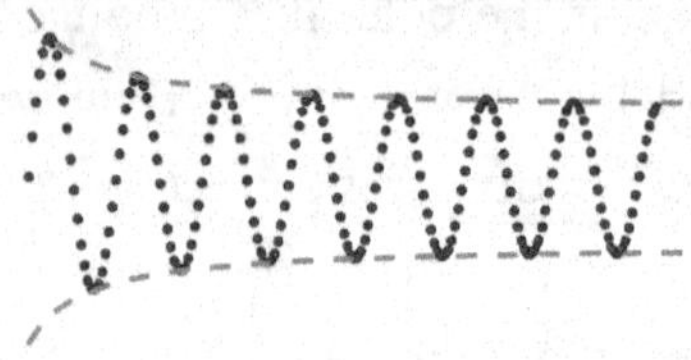

"And then, Susan put together that DFT sequence that let us map that out in the Z dimension like a helix, that was an extra dimension added to the Fibonacci spiral. So, when George and I set it up as a displacement array modulating our high-energy wavefield, it produced a resonant coupling effect kind of like resonant inductive coupling."

She wrote the sequence on the whiteboard.

0, 1, 1, 2, 3, 5, 8, 13, 21, 34

"...And that worked pretty much as planned, which is great. It lets us energize specific portions of the field using non-radiative electromagnetic energy resonant tunneling. But the effect we're seeing here is much more than that. We've got a high-energy accelerated energy field resonating with *something* on a quantum level."

"So, we're creating resonant vibrations in this fabric, you might say. And then we accelerate and modulate that field, and it responds in a way that is very, very interesting."

"As opposed to the old particle-specific approach," added Erich.

He sketched out a diagram of wavefield interactions with a blue marker.

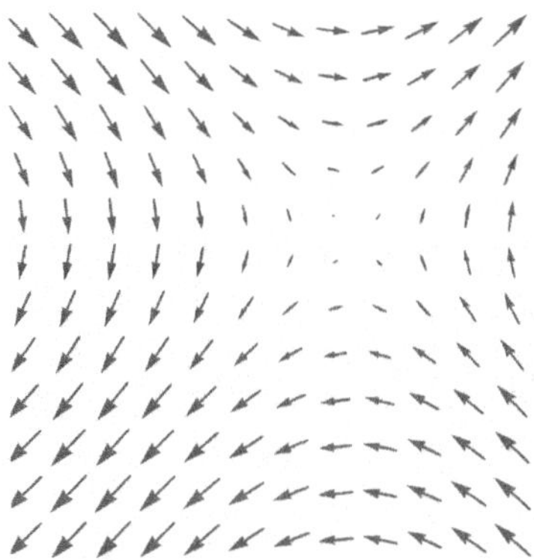

"So that's the interesting thing. The analog wavefield is exactly what we were trying to model with a digital sampling sort of approach. We never really captured the essence until we began transforming the analog wavefields directly. That's why we needed that vector field firmware in there."

"Okay, so, let's backup this new stuff and get out of here," said Erich. "Is this board okay to clean?"

"Yep, go ahead. I've got it," said Amir, taking one last photo of the whiteboard. Rössler disconnected his laptop from the video input to the big screen and closed the lid, then packed it into his briefcase before wiping the whiteboard clean.

Susan minimized her on-screen window to reveal a project management worksheet. She stared at it for a few seconds then said to Karl, "We really have no idea what this new firmware is, right? Should we test it before downgrading?"

"Uh, I assumed it was the new firmware we tried a few days ago." Realization flickered across Karl's expression. "Oh, so it might not be? Wait—I can check that."

He typed a couple of commands into the shell. "Hey, holy smoke, you're right. The checksum is different and the version number is different. It rewrote itself entirely in that 12.38-hour period. That was *fast*."

"We can't have it rewriting itself until we figure out what's going on." noted Erich.

"I already did that," Karl reminded him. "I disabled the automated executive controller. The version control library updater is strictly manual at this point."

"Yeah, and the other you that *didn't* jump forward in time has probably fixed all the bugs," teased Li Yan. "What would Karl do?"

"No, there is no other Karl. Karl's been out of the picture

completely for this entire 15 hours. Mrs. Schraeder is not going to be pleased," said Karl with a smirk.

"Come on you guys," Li Yan said, only half-jokingly. "We need to get *backwards* time travel working. I need *more* hours per day, not less. Then I could have three extra hours of sleep. And maybe then I'd get all my work done on time. "I don't know for sure, though. I've never had three extra hours, hey?"

"Uh, well, yah, we should do a full disassembly—a proper one, you know—before we do anything different. I'm not sure we'd have another chance."

"And we should have a full backup of our magic software/firmware combination moved into secure storage before we start, just to be safe."

"I'll take that," offered George.

"Li, can you do a diagnostic dump of the new firmware to figure out the dependencies and all that?"

Li Yan nodded as she typed. "*Before* we run it, next time, please?" She hit the Enter key. "It shouldn't take long." She smiled. "In fact, it's done already."

"Okay," said Karl, watching the terminal output window. "Backup is at 55%...89%... Firmware backup is complete."

Everyone looked at George. "Uh, 5 hours and 59 minutes to go, give or take."

Erich closed the latches on his briefcase then lifted his jacket from the coat hook and put it on. "Go home, get a good night's sleep. We'll start fresh in the morning, yes?"

Susan and Amir had already removed their lab coats and were sweeping cans and juice boxes off the table into a recycling bin.

Amir straightened the small stack of paper he had filled with notes and tucked the stack into a clear plastic envelope.

"Take good care of those. We'll need those tomorrow."

Karl was still typing. "You too, Karl. Come on, shoo." Erich and Karl caught up to them as the group waited for the elevator. "I'll be here at 8," Erich said. The door opened. "You go ahead. I have two things to do. George, if there is anything else you need to have done with the backup, please have it complete by then. Okay? Great. I will see you all in the control center at 8 a.m. sharp. Bye bye." When the door closed, Erich watched the display change from L1 to M. He pulled a key ring with a small key out of his pocket and pressed the call button.

When the elevator got to the main floor, everyone in the group except George exited and made their way past the empty front desk and self-serve kiosk area to the front doors.

"Um, I'm parked below," said George. "I'll see you folks tomorrow."

"Good luck with that backup, Geo," said Karl.

George walked past the elevator area and headed down the hall in the opposite direction from the parking level elevator.

As he passed the elevator, the display showed the elevator was heading down to L1. George hustled past and quickly swiped his card to let himself into the server room.

Inside the elevator, Erich inserted a small key into the elevator control panel. He turned the key and pressed the "4" button. The doors closed.

George stood next to a terminal mounted next to a rack of high-performance blade servers in the MPAS computing cluster area. He pulled a portable hard drive from his pocket and connected it.

Outside in the parking lot, Li Yan was chatting with Susan when Karl's car pulled up. The driver's side window rolled down and Karl leaned out. "Hey, we're going for a couple of drinks. Wanna come along?"

○ ○ ○

At the local bar, Li Yan, Karl, Susan, and Amir sat in one of the semicircular booths.

"What's the deal with AIMG?" asked Susan.

"You know the name stands for Advanced Innovations Marketing Group," said Li Yan from across the table. She leaned forward and, in a quieter voice, said: "That's Stern. Do you know how he got the company off the ground? When he was a professor, he set up an innovations incubator at the university, in which students developed various innovative products and services. There were several e-business platforms launched, the whole AI program got started there, some cloud computing stuff and whatnot. He set it up as a numbered company—just a dummy corporation, really—and patented several of these inventions by the students. And then sold the patents to the dummy corporation, which he owned. And the students essentially got nothing. A job, maybe, if they are lucky. No profit sharing at all. He basically patented their ideas and screwed them out of their intellectual property rights."

"Nice guy," said Amir, raising his nearly empty beer glass in a mock toast.

"He's a creep," said Li. "He comes around occasionally."

"I think Rössler's scared of him," added Karl. He looked at Susan. "Don't you?"

"I dunno. I thought maybe Rössler was working from the same playbook. We've all signed NDAs, right?"

"Yeah, you know George? He was one of Stern's students back then. He was pissed when Stern patented his Cherenkov compensator. I think he's still got a bit of a chip on his shoulder."

Amir finished his beer. "Anyone having another?" he asked.

"I've gotta go."

"Yah, me too."

"Okay, see you in—ooh—eight hours."

"Goodnight."

o o o

In Stern's office on the 4th floor, Stern shook Rössler's hand. On the corner of Stern's desk sat a small hard drive. "Thank you, Erich. I'll have this taken care of right away. Keep up the good work."

o o o

6

A Giant Leap

Susan's phone buzzed. It was a text from Richard Rutherford.

Hey night owl. How was your first week?

It always began this way. She'd reply. He'd say something sweet. Then some outrageous offer. They'd had fun in Mexico, though.

Amazing. We might have even had a breakthrough the other day. Do you still believe that wavefunctions aren't real at all?

Beware: this is a QM researcher's idea of sexy talk.

:)

I think it is position, momentum, and so on, that are the reality.

What about wavefunction collapse?

Decoherence is not the same as collapse. So it's going well then?

Mostly good. We experienced an unexpected ripple effect while running the accelerator recently. Still wondering why....

Was there a ring of light visible during the ripple phase?

We didn't see one.

Probably not Cherenkov Radiation. Shouldn't happen in vacuum. Maybe Casimir Effect?

Could it be Alcubierre field?

With or without exotic matter?

Without, most likely.

Maybe using Casimir Effect to fulfill negative energy requirement. It's been theorized. Should see a ring of light. If so, could be Perturbative M-Theory effects. You'd like those.

Getting late, must go. Thanks for ideas.

Hugs, S.

10 minutes later another text message arrived.

I have a nice surprise for you. Can I come over?

Susan looked at the clock. It was quarter to one. This is the way it starts.

Rich, she wrote, erased, and wrote again. I appreciate everything you've done for me. I'm sorry, but I need to move on.

She tapped Send, instantly regretting her choice of words.

A moment later the phone rang. "Let me just drop off this nice surprise I have for you," he said. So typical.

"Richard, to be clear: No, thank you. I can't continue in this relationship. I have to break this off *now*. I cannot see you again. I hope you understand. Good*bye*."

She cringed a little as she ended the call. The finality hung in the air for a moment and then her mood lifted. She exhaled and she felt better. It felt much better now.

∘ ∘ ∘

The next morning, Susan arrived at the quad early and stopped into the kitchen for a bottle of water on the way to the L101 conference room. Li Yan was pouring a coffee and Karl was gabbing with Erich about the day's schedule.

"Have you seen Amir?"

"He said he'd be down in the control center," said Erich.

Susan slipped the water bottle into her labcoat pocket. "Great, I'll head down there now."

"Karl and I will run the sequence from my office," said Erich. "Can you and Amir help Li Yan with the local diagnostics? She's in the control room down there."

"Sure."

"Are we all ready, Li?" Erich said into the speakerphone, looking at the clock on the wall. It was 7:55.

"Roger that, boss. Diagnostics are online and running. Ready when you are."

"George says he's just about ready for us," confirmed Karl.

Ping.

"Okay, George says they're all ready. Susan?"

"Amir and I are on the floor at the field monitor station. Monitors are live."

"All right, everyone," said Erich. "All aboard for the flight of the Fibonacci. Today's our first test of the new software."

"All systems are go. Let's run the full sequence."

"Dynamic resequencing is... complete."

"All right folks, here we go."

The electromagnetic array hummed.

Karl read the status markers as they flashed onto the dashboard display.

"0, 1, 1, 2, 3, 5, 8, 13, 21, 34..."

A ripple disturbed the surface of Susan's water bottle and the intercom speaker clicked. Across the hall, some lights flipped off.

"Power failure?"

"No, no I don't think so. Just some lights turning off, I think."

"Whoa. Look at the clock."

Amir poked at his cell phone. "Weird," he mumbled.

Susan picked up the receiver and pressed the Speaker button on the desk phone. "Hello... Erich?" She tapped the hang-up button twice, then again. "Dammit, he hung up." She handed the receiver to Amir. "Can you get Rössler on the phone?"

"I'll try," said Amir. "My phone seems to be acting up." Amir picked up the desk phone and tapped in the shortcode for Rössler's office on the desk phone. He listened for the ring tone, then handed the receiver to Susan.

"Yah?"

"Erich."

"Who's this?"

"It's Susan."

"Susan...Everett?" She heard a rustling noise, then "Hey! Hey guys, it's Susan! Susan Everett!" The voice came back to full volume. "Where's Amir? Are you okay?"

"He's here. We're down at the field monitor station. Yeah, we're fine."

She heard Erich in the background speaking to someone else. "Yes! Susan Everett... and Amir Roy!"

Erich's voice returned to full volume. "Wow," he said. "You're back. Exactly as predicted. Nice work."

"I never left."

"Well, we have *much* to talk about, don't we?" said Erich.

Susan heard other voices talking in the background. "Erich...Erich! What's going on?"

"Stay there," he said, sounding distracted. "We're coming right down there."

Minutes later, Susan and Amir sat with Erich in his office. Amir aligned the wood-and-brass "E Rössler" sign with the pattern on his desk.

"How long has it been?"

"It's been five years."

Susan turned to Amir in disbelief. "Five years!"

"Actually 5.05, to be more precise."

Amir suddenly felt sick to his stomach.

Erich unfolded his hands and made a clockwise gesture. "You know, that was the very first big test. We fixed lots of bugs since. We weren't really sure if you'd come back. On time, I mean."

She shook her head. "Where is George Gunderson?"

"George has left the company. I'm actually not at liberty to discuss the specific reasons why, sorry."

Susan crossed her arms on the desk. Erich was avoiding eye contact.

"We'll explain everything we can, as soon as possible."

"Why can't you explain it *now?*"

"We're still investigating. We ask for your patience. Please."

Erich pressed down a button labeled 'Security' on the phone console.

As he held down the button, the audio from the office was transmitted to and recorded by the security desk. At the desk, one of the two guards responded by getting up and heading for the stairs. The other silenced the flashing yellow alert and pressed his thumb on the security console's biometric sensor to take over management of the console.

"We must have a doctor examine you both immediately. We need to do that now."

Amir looked apprehensively at Susan.

"You want a female doctor, yes?" Erich said to Susan.

"I think I want some answers first. And I need to use a phone. Mine doesn't work."

"We'll do that right after we get a doctor to examine you both, okay? Sit right over here. The doc on the way."

"1202. One male and one female," said the guard into his handset.

"Roger that."

"On our way," said the guard into his handset as he led a man and a woman up the stairwell. They each carried a neatly folded white lab coat. The man also carried a small tray.

"This way," he said as he swiped his card at the 1st floor stairwell door and led them up the stairs.

o o o

Erich was growing impatient. "I'll be right back."

As soon as Erich left the room, he raised his mobile phone to his ear and spoke angrily. "Where *are* they?"

"They are on their way now, sir."

Erich took a deep breath and swallowed. "Good. Send them over as soon as they get here," he said in a calm and measured tone. He leaned close to the security guard. "And keep an eye on those two."

At the security desk, the guard opened a drawer with a pad of micro-thin SIM chips and pulled off one of the adhesive disks. With a pair of fine-tipped tweezers, he peeled one off and set it upside down next to another one already on the plate.

As the man and woman—now wearing their white lab coats—approached the security desk, he slid the plate toward them. The man placed the plate on the tray, and nodded at the guard. The pair then headed for Rössler's office.

Moments later, Erich ushered Amir and Susan into his office. "Please have a seat." He handed them each a new security badge. Each was in a clear plastic case with a small metallic clip. On the backside of each card was one of the small adhesive disks.

"Here you go, Amir—new security badges for you and Susan. Just give me your old security badges—they have expired." Suddenly, his cell phone rang. "Just a sec...."

Amir unclipped his old ID card. Susan watched Erich as he left the room, talking quietly.

Then there were other voices outside the door. Erich opened it. "Here they are," he gestured with his phone to the two doctors. "Susan, you'll be in that room, through that door there. Okay. I'll be outside while they're checking you."

He closed the office door.

The woman directed Susan to the adjoining room. "Please remove all your clothes and put on this gown...."

○ ○ ○

The door to the adjoining room opened a crack and Susan peeked into the office where Amir was undressing. "*Psst.*" Like her, Amir had been allowed some privacy while disrobing. At this point, his shirt, shoes and pants were off. His face flushed when he saw her looking at him. Susan, still fully clothed, entered the room and pulled at his arm. "Grab your clothes, quick. Come on."

"Wait—what?"

"Let's go down to the door and *test* these badges our*selves.*" She tugged a little harder, pulling him into the joining room. "Right now. Come *on.*"

Amir pulled his pants on, quietly protesting. "Are you just being paranoid?"

"No. Trust me." Susan peeked around the corner. Rössler and the doctors were near his office door, facing the other way. "Okay," she whispered. "This way...."

He followed her as she hurried to the stairwell next to the office.

"You want to know why I don't believe them? Look at this." Susan held her phone in front of him inside the stairwell. It was a message from George.

"They are going to inject tracking bugs into your arm. Don't let them stick a needle in you!" She waved the card on its lanyard. "And why do you think they are trying to take these cards away? These cards work on the elevator, and the other doors. Right? I'll betcha they work with *all* the doors. That's why they wanted to take them away."

Amir was going to point out that they could undoubtedly disable these cards any time they wanted to, but Rössler *did* seem to be unusually interested in swapping out the cards.

"Stay here. And don't let this door close," she said. She walked into the lobby and casually swiped her card at the elevator. Nothing. The security desk camera silently recorded as she tried again. Damn. No good. As she walked quickly back to the stairwell door, Amir held up his card. "They are probably tracking these cards," he said.

Seconds later, two security guards rushed into the lobby.

Amir and Susan were nowhere to be seen.

7

A New Identity

Amir stood in an empty parking spot on P1. "It's been stolen."

Susan dared to be a little hopeful. "Maybe just towed or moved. It's been more than five years, after all." Suddenly it sunk in. "God—I've gotta get in touch with my mom! She must be worried *sick*. I've gotta go over there."

"Do you have a car here?" asked Amir.

"I sure hope so," said Susan. "I parked it down on P2. Come on...."

They ran to the door. Susan pulled it open... and the two security guards were standing there.

"Woah, we were *so* lost—thanks!" bluffed Susan.

The security guard on Susan's left spoke into his mic. "1202. Male and female have been located in P1, over."

Susan turned to the guard. "Can you guys look into his missing car, please? That *is* part of your job, right?"

The guard looked at his partner.

Susan pressed harder on the point. "You must have records of towed and abandoned vehicles, yes?"

The other spoke into his mic. "1202, requesting vehicle records." He turned to Amir. "What are the plates and what is the make of the vehicle, sir?"

"Plates. Yeah. Um, plate is DD8-A15. It's a Mazda3."

"1202, we're looking for plate ID of Delta Delta Eight, Alpha One Five. That's a Mazda three, over."

o o o

Once again, Amir and Susan found themselves sitting in Erich's office.

"That was very naughty, you guys. You know, you're not prisoners here. We're just trying to *take care* of you. We're looking for your car, Amir. And Susan, did you get through to that number you were trying to reach?"

"No, I didn't. It's my mom—I'm just trying to let her know I'm okay. She must be worried sick. I've gotta go over there."

"Susan," began Erich, in an uncharacteristically sympathetic tone, "I hate to have to say this, but *please* remember that you and Amir both signed non-disclosure agreements specifically forbidding you from discussing *any* aspect of our research to members of your family or anyone else. Given that you haven't aged a day in more than five years, is that going to be a problem?"

Susan bit her tongue and nodded. "No sir. I understand."

"Were you parked downstairs, too?"

"Uh huh. I parked in the secured area of the parking

garage—on P2. I don't recall the spot number, though. Can I take a look?"

"I'd like to go, too," added Amir.

"Yes, you're both free to go *provided* that you both come back here tomorrow for debriefing. I know you guys will need some money." He gave them each a hundred-dollar bill. "We'll get you fixed up properly tomorrow. This is all I've got right now. Try not to spend it all, okay? Be careful out there."

They thanked him and got up to leave. He looked up at them over the top of his glasses. "I'm very glad you're back. It's been a long time."

He seemed to hesitate for a few seconds and then said, "I'll see you to the elevator."

o o o

Erich swiped each card on the elevator's card reader. "Okay, these cards are working now," he said. If you don't want to allow us to do a blood test, at least you'll need a working card to enter the building." He pressed L1 on the elevator controller's touchscreen, then pulled a pen and a couple of business cards out of his shirt pocket. "I really don't feel too good about you guys going out alone, but I suppose I can't stop you."

He wrote a phone number on each card and handed them the cards as the elevator doors opened. "Look, here's my mobile number, he said. "Call me if you have problems with *anything*. Anything at all. I'll be home after 7 p.m. We'll try to get some new jobs for you tomorrow, okay?"

Susan studied the logo on the card with a rising sense of alienation.

"A division of *Andna*. What's Andna?"

"Oh, that's the new corporate identity. New logo. We're multinational now," he said proudly, looking at Amir as if would have special significance to him.

○ ○ ○

P2

Susan stood next to the light blue Toyota Camry she got from her mom. "Well, at least my car is still here." Susan ran her finger over the window.

"Omigod," said Amir. "It's absolutely filthy."

She turned the key in the ignition. Nothing.

"Bah. So much for that plan. Come on, let's find a bus and go to the bank. Have you got any small bills or change?"

"I dunno. Maybe five or ten and some change."

"Could you look, please?" Susan was getting annoyed at his space cadet routine. "I really need you to to pull it together Amir, okay?"

"Sorry, sorry," he mumbled. "Um, they don't take cash."

"Hmm?"

"The buses. They don't take cash."

"Oh, bloody hell. Forget that. We'll find a taxi."

She rifled through her wallet.

"Ugh, my credit cards have expired."

"The cards don't work?"

"Grr," grumbled Susan. "Even the debit cards."

"It's a freakin' nightmare."

Amir's state of mind was veering from traumatized to morose.

"Why do debit cards even *have* an expiration date?"

Amir didn't respond. Visibly shaken, he emptied his pockets and stared blankly at the car key and crumpled papers in his hands. When a security guard approached, he held the hand with the key toward him.

"Did you find out anything about my car? Has it been found?"

"We're still looking, sir," said the guard. "What's your full name and phone number? We'll let you know as soon as we have some more information about it."

"Uhh, Amir Roy," he stammered. "But... my–my phone's not working. I've got no service."

Susan handed the guard the card with Rössler's number. "Phone that number when you find his car."

Amir stared blankly at his non-functional phone. "I can't reach anyone."

"Me neither," said Susan. "Come on. We'll get new phones or SIMs or whatever...."

Just then, a driver pulled up in a dark blue van. It was a type of vehicle neither of them recognized. Its unusual LED lights glared in the dim light. As the driver-side window slid down, he leaned out. "Hey, car trouble?"

"Yeah, thanks for stopping! It's a dead battery, I think," said Susan. "I have some jumper cables in my trunk. Can you give us a jump start?"

"You want to try jumpin' it?"

"Yes please!"

Amir's mood improved immediately. "You're a lifesaver," he said.

The young man popped the hood of his van. With gloved hands, he lifted the hood and pulled open a plastic cover, exposing a pair of familiar looking connection points marked with [+] and [–] signs. Susan handed him the red and black jumper cables.

"Heh, it's the first time I've ever used these 'low voltage' terminals," he confessed. "Ah, right, there's positive and negative symbols here." He connected the clips and looked at Susan. "It's funny: I can charge phones and all things USB, but I've never tried charging a car."

"Oh, we don't need a charge," said Amir. "Just enough power to turn over our engine a few times will be plenty, thanks."

"I admit I haven't even been under the hood of this thing since I got it. And that was ages ago. I don't have especially high-tech requirements. It just had to get me here from Western Canada. And even *that* can be a challenge in an electric vehicle."

He watched as Susan opened her car's hood.

"Ah, who am I kidding? I hate this van, really. LIDAR and cameras and GPS and sensors and AI, and man, I really don't want anything to do with any of that *crap*. And you know what the absolute *worst* feature of all is? The battery for this vehicle is under the hood here in the front, right? And this hood latch is battery operated! So if my battery dies, I can't even get to it! Unbelievable. You're lucky to have a manual hood release."

With a cable in each hand, he waited as Susan propped up her car's hood. "But I do know how to do this." He peered at her car's battery. "Just pull those plastic things away from the terminals," he suggested to Susan.

You have the gloves, she thought as she pulled up the plastic covers.

Susan looked at the white buildup on the negative electrode and the even ghastlier-looking green-and-blue muck covering the positive terminal. "That's a sad lookin' battery."

"Here, I can help," said Amir. He scraped the blue-green buildup from the positive terminal. "Copper sulfate," he mumbled. "And these gray-white crystals are sulfate. Yuck."

Susan got behind the wheel and rolled down her window. "So that's an electric van, huh?"

"Yeah, it's a bit old, but it still holds a charge. And your car runs on gas? Wow. Old school."

A moment later, Susan's car was running. Susan flashed a big smile at his 'thumbs up' gesture.

"Be sure to drive it for a while to charge up that battery properly, heh?" he said.

Susan closed the hood. "Thanks a lot. I owe you one."

"No problem. I'm kinda new here. It's always nice to meet someone." He got into the van and leaned out the open window. "My name's Andrew. See ya around, I hope."

"Susan," she said. "Bye Andrew, thanks again."

"Pardon me for asking, Andrew," said Amir, "but are you heading toward town?"

"Yeah, I live close to downtown, near the Mill Hill turnoff."

"Oh, perfect—I'm down Market Street, right past there. Do you think I could catch a ride there with you?"

"Yeah, sure," said Andrew.

I've gotta go," said Susan, behind the wheel again.

Amir put a hand on the open window frame. "Will you be okay?"

She buckled her seat belt. "Yes, thanks, I'm going to go over to my mom's place."

Amir looked at Susan. "Can you pick me up at my place at, say, 4 o'clock?"

"Okay. I'll pick you up at the bus stop on the northeast corner of Mercer and Market at 4 p.m."

"Perfect."

Susan noticed the date sticker on Andrew's license plate and the Earth First bumper sticker. 'Oh right,' she thought to herself. 'My automobile insurance expired five years ago. I'll have to take care of that first.'

Andrew stepped back from her car. "So, you're good to go, I guess. Maybe I'll see you at the office?"

"Yeah thanks again. We're on Dr. Rössler's team, in the MPAS lab. So maybe we'll see you around?" She caught his eye and flashed him a smile, wondering which department he worked in.

"I hope so," he said, then turned and climbed into the driver's seat. Amir got in the passenger side. "Good luck!"

Susan pulled her car out of the parking garage and onto the street, feeling a little guilty about all the carbon monoxide fumes she had left behind in the parking garage.

"Ready to go?" asked Andrew, buckling his seat belt.

"Sure, thanks."

Andrew and Amir followed her blue Camry as they left the parking garage and headed down the street past the mini-mall on the corner. All three of the stores that used to be there—an electronics store, a restaurant and a donut shop—appeared to be out of business.

Amir looked at the paper-covered windows and 'For Lease' signs as they drove down the pike. In the next block was another mall—also shuttered. "Good grief, it's a ghetto around here. When did the mall close?"

"Oh, that closed just after I moved here, about a year ago.

The anchor retailers pulled out first and then the whole mall clientele really dropped off. Well, the mall business was already having a rough time due to internet sales, of course."

Andrew pointed to a big building up ahead. "But this big automall coming up here on the right seems to be doing okay. And they say the luxury markets are doing quite well. So, there's money out there."

Andrew noticed the badge on the lanyard around Amir's neck. "So, you work at the lab there, eh?"

Amir shrugged. "Sort of. I'm an intern."

"I came down here from Canada," said Andrew. "Were you born here?"

"No, I came with my older sister from Mumbai about ten years ago," replied Amir. "I'm a friend of Susan's," he added, hoping Andrew would give up on this line of questioning.

"Those old cars can be a pain in the butt, eh?"

"Yeah, I hope she's okay," he said absently, chilled by the sudden realization of the improbability of his possessions still being in *his* apartment.

o o o

Four hours later, Rössler was still in the lab with Li Yan and Karl when his cellphone rang.

He covered the microphone with his hand. "It's Susan."

She sounded stressed.

"Do you know how hard it is to find a cell phone provider that accepts cash around here? No, no, we finally found one. We're sharing one phone for now. I've just been informed that my social security number is 'dormant,' someone else is living in Amir's apartment and no one seems to know what happened to all his possessions. Yeah, he's here. The tax department has frozen all my accounts. I've been driving around all day in an uninsured car. And no one explained anything to the police when my mother reported me missing!?"

"I'm sorry. We weren't allowed to. As I'm sure you know, a great many law enforcement agencies, government regulators, and news organizations get involved as soon as a missing persons report is filed. We really didn't think that was a prudent step, considering the non-public nature of our research—not to mention the incredible scope of the breakthrough that you and Amir seem to have just witnessed first-hand. We're still analyzing the data and we need to do some medical tests on you both, to understand exactly what we're dealing with here."

"Medical tests? What did those doctors find? Do you have any reason to believe they may be medical issues or any sorts of side effects?"

"I know it sound ridiculous to say this after five years, but it's really too soon to say. There haven't been *any* other long-term test subjects like yourselves, who have made multiple jumps. And honestly, for legal reasons, we haven't done any more long-term human tests, period."

Susan looked skeptically at Amir. "I think we're fine. Uh huh. Yeah, I think I can sort all that stuff out. Okay. Thanks."

"Where are you now?"

"We're in the drive-through line of—what is the name here? —some burger joint. Yeah, I know, well... we were hungry. And we didn't want to turn off the engine. It's a long story. Yeah, he's with me."

"I'm not sure. Maybe a motel. Yeah, we got it straightened out at the bank. I'll tell you all about it in the morning. Sure, 9 o'clock. Okay. Thanks."

o o o

At the Green Door Motel, Amir opened the door and sniffed a little. "So, you're okay with sharing this room with me?"

"Yes Amir," said Susan, throwing her backpack onto the queen-size bed as she headed into the bathroom. "We'll be fine."

"Are you...uh, should I sleep on the couch?"

"I dunno," said Susan. "Where would you *like* to sleep?" A part of her wanted Amir to step up his game. But Amir was polite, as always. He demurred to the couch.

Minutes later, Susan was on the phone again. "Did you call your family?" she asked Amir.

"No, said Amir. They're in Mumbai and—Omigod! —the international rates are crazy here. I don't really talk with them very often. It's okay. What about you?"

"Well, I live with my mom. But she's not answering her phone. I'm a bit worried, to be honest."

She absent-mindedly rotated Rössler's business card under her fingers as she thought about what to do.

"We should go over there. Would that be okay with you? I'd really like to see if she's all right."

When they arrived, the apartment was filled with boxes. Mattresses and box-springs leaned up against the wall.

The first thing Susan did was check her mom's answering machine. The telephone system's message log was full, but Susan gleaned enough information from the condolences and funeral enquiries to learn that her mother had recently died.

"You lived here with your mother?"

"Yes, she was getting a bit frail, and she had an extra room. I was going to school, so it worked out pretty well for me."

"I'm really sorry."

"I can't believe that I've been missing—gone, might as well be dead—for five years and apparently no one but the tax department noticed."

"What about all the bills?"

"They were handled via automatic payments. She sold the house after my father died."

"I guess you could stay here," suggested Amir.

"Oh god, no. No way." She wasn't ready for wills or being in probate or any of that.

Susan called Erich. "I'd like to volunteer for the next round of tests."

Erich sounded tired. "We'll talk about it in the morning. Susan... in the morning. Yes, I'll be there at 9 a.m. See you then."

o o o

8

Big Time

Erich Rössler was talking with Karl at five to nine. "For one thing, it's obvious that we need to fully quantify the algorithm for time-jumping. And, we need to start testing if the results we've seen to date in validating the potential for reverse-time displacement are indicative of the values we can expect to see at different power-stepping values."

Rössler saw Susan, Amir and a security guard step out of the elevator. "There you are! Dear me, you look upset, Susan. Are you okay?"

"Not really."

Amir followed, carrying a small suitcase.

Susan slung the backpack off her back and set it beside her on the ground. "Luckily the superstore is open late. This is everything I own. I've literally lost everything."

"You too, Amir?"

"I don't know yet. Maybe."

"All his stuff is gone," said Susan grimly. He looked sullen for a moment, then blurted out, "I want to go back."

"Well, Amir, we don't know how to do that yet. Just calm down."

That rankled him further. "You know that telling a person to calm down *never* works, right?"

"Sorry. Look, we've put all plans for further testing on hold while we try to figure this out."

"Well, send me forward again then. I don't want to wait around while you figure it out. I just want to get back to my own time."

"Patience, please. There are some things that are really important that we need to review with you. And maybe you can help us with some things, too."

"Like what?"

Karl pulled up a spreadsheet. "Well, this is interesting: in the first test, we all jumped approximately 17.25 seconds. Then we jumped roughly 12.38 hours. The numbers aren't exact, because they're on a curve. See? It's the Fibonacci cumulative value—the total of our test sequence numbers."

The spreadsheet displayed the rounded values of the irrational numeric sequence.

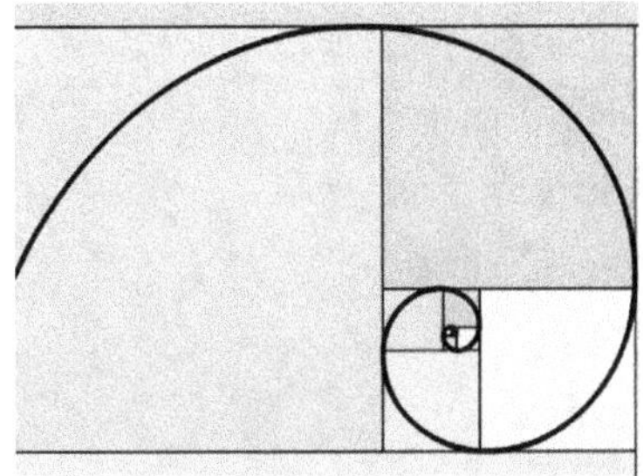

[Fibonacci sequence value n] * 17.25 seconds [displacement unit value] / 60 [seconds], /60 [minutes], /24 [hours], /365 [days].

n * 17.25 /60 /60 /24 /365

"0, 1, 1, 2, 3, 5, 8, 13, 21, 34..."

"Ah yes, I see," said Susan.

"Here," said Karl, I'll send you the sequence I calculated with some bigger values...."

0, 1, 1, 2, 3, 5, 8, 13, 21, 34, 55, 89, 144, 233, 377, 610, 987, 1597, 2584, 4181, 6765

0   (Fn 0)

1 = 17.25 seconds

1 = 17.25 seconds

2 = 34.5 seconds

3 = 51.75 seconds

5 = 86.25 seconds

8 = 2.3 minutes

13 = 3.74 minutes

21 = 6.04 minutes

34 = 9.78 minutes

55 = 15.81 minutes   (Fn 10)

89 = 25.59 minutes

144 = 41.4 minutes

233 = 66.99 minutes

377 = 1.81 hours

610 = 2.92 hours

987 = 4.73 hours

1597 = 7.65 hours

2584 = 12.38 hours

4181 = 20.03 hours

6765 = 32.42 hours   (Fn 20)

10946 = 2.19 days

17711 = 3.54 days

28657 = 5.72 days

46368 = 9.26 days

75025 = 14.98 days

121393 = 24.24 days

196418 = 39.22 days

317811 = 63.45 days

514229 = 102.67 days

832040 = 166.12 days (Fn 30)

1346269 = 268.79 days

2178309 = 434.91 days

3524578 = 1.93 years

5702887 = 3.12 years

9227465 = 5.05 years

14930352 = 8.17 years

24157817 = 13.21 years

39088169 = 21.38 years

63245986 = 34.6 years

102334155 = 55.98 years   (Fn 40)

165580141 = 90.57 years
267914296 = 146.55 years
433494437 = 237.12 years
701408733 = 383.67 years
1134903170 = 620.79 years
1836311903 = 1004.45 years
2971215073 = 1625.24 years
4807526976 = 2629.69 years
7778742049 = 4254.92 years
12586269025 = 6884.61 years   (Fn 50)

"As you can see, those numbers will get very big, very fast, as we step through the sequence."

"Hey, why don't you guys crash at my place tonight?" suggested Li Yan.

"Sure," said Susan.

"Yeah that sounds great," said Amir. "Thanks."

"Okay," said Dr. Rössler. "See you all here for the meeting tomorrow morning at 10 a.m."

That night, Li Yan opened a bottle of red wine and they all toasted to a much better tomorrow.

o o o

"Big news," proclaimed Erich the next day. "The board has approved the release of some information about this pioneering work. We're only going to disclose the results from the first two short-term tests, though, to minimize controversy. And those are the ones we all went through. We're going to be famous, folks."

"But I'm not telling people I went forward with you. The glory is yours. I don't want to take away from that." Dr. Rössler moved closer to inspect their faces. "You look okay. Do you feel all right?"

Amir nodded. Susan raised her eyebrows. "What are we pioneering? Surely you've done other tests in the past eight years?"

"Yes of course, but nothing big. Nothing like this. Just little tests, lots of little ones. We had a few problems," he conceded. "But you two—this is the real success."

In an office on the third floor, a young man with a very old hand typed on a computer keyboard. "No more refugees" said the screen. It was Andrew.

o o o

"All right," said Susan. "I'd like to talk about what we need for the next jump. We hit snags with credit cards. And car batteries."

"I'm sorry," said Erich. "We are pretty organized these days, but we messed up on that one. We have some of what you'll need already prepared. We have a briefing program that keeps flash-forwarders like yourselves on top of important changes in policies, world events, and so on. Does that sound like it might be interesting to you?"

"Yeah, I guess so. Is this briefing program a meeting of some sort, or an online thing?"

"Both are available. The orientation session is an in-person briefing, like a seminar. Couple of hundred people, max."

"A couple of hundred!? How many are jumping these days?"

"There are several international programs at this point. "We're only handling U.S. citizens here, and a few visa holders with highly specialized technical skills—our man Karl here, for example."

Karl smiled uneasily. This was the first Susan, Li Yan or Amir had heard about his interest in making a jump.

"Okay, there's an orientation meeting for prospective jumpers at 9 a.m. this coming Thursday, downstairs in L106 —the big room. They do a virus screening, too, so you should only go if you're feeling well. Can you and Amir make that, Susan?"

Susan looked at Amir. He shrugged. "Yeah, sure."

Erich looked at his phone and furrowed his brow. "You'll also need to bring some picture ID. I won't be there, but they will take care of you. Anything else?"

"Mostly, this time, we really need to ensure that our cars will not get towed away or broken into," said Susan. Amir nodded vigorously.

"For sure. We already took some of those steps for your car this time, Susan. I registered it with the Security Desk with a non-expiring 'do not remove' permit. But really, these days, it's easier and safer to use an on-demand vehicle."

"So, how long is this 'non-expiring' pass likely to be good for?"

"Heh. Well, presumably, that pass *should* be good for as long as the company (or its successor) exists."

"All right," said Susan, "I'd like to do a bigger jump—go a few decades ahead. Can we do that?"

"The problem with those long jumps, of course," noted Erich, "is that the digital stuff doesn't scale well past a couple of years. Passwords expire, accounts go dormant, security certificates, cellular standards, and whatnot.

"It doesn't scale well, so we have a rule—sort of a guiding principle—that those who do time jumps need a certain amount of reorientation when they get to their destination, you know? We've found that reintegration counseling is practically an essential service after longer jumps. There are just so many little things that can expire or go wrong..."

"Yeah, tell me about it," said Amir.

"Like your car, Amir. Really sorry about that. We eventually found out that was stolen, but we were never able to successfully retrieve it. But we do have an insurance system mostly in place now, to minimize the impact of these sorts of things."

"I think the big problem with those long jumps," Susan argued, "is that you guys—and everyone else in the program—are getting older than we are. Is there a business and technical continuity plan fully in place?"

"Well, I'd have to say yes to this, with some caveats. We've set up a tracking program to keep track of all jumpers, when they left, how far ahead they jumped. We then block out that arrival time for all future travelers, to reduce the risk of arrival-time overlaps. We provide them with ID that proves they are who they say they are and hopefully will help to mitigate any problems that may arise when they show up on someone else's property without warning. We've established strict guidelines that should allow us to pass messages forward to registered jumpers, and also pass alerts on to authorities, in case of criminal or terrorist activity, or the introduction of a potentially dangerous contagion. It's a difficult problem: we can't be sure they're received a message and one of our jumpers might end up landing on someone's private property, so we felt this level of rigor gave us the best chance of success. It is the jumper's responsibility to establish a relationship with whoever lives or works at that future location. The jumpers must prove to those people that they are the intended recipient of the information or packages we're sending. We just have to trust that some of them will be forwarded from those jump-points if the jumpers continue on moving forward into the future. And we have to get indemnification releases, of course our legal department requires this.

"We are always trying to improve. We've had a pretty good run these five years, thanks in large part to Li Yan and Karl here. However...."

He paused and rubbed his eyes. He looked tired.

"The technology—the jumping only forward in time— has proven difficult for the company to monetize in really meaningful ways, and funds for the program are sometimes ... a bit challenging to get everything we need. Time-shifted perishables and other age deferrals, of course, have some value, particularly to those at the receiving end of the jump. So that's not great for monetization, but not impossible either. It tends to be a disadvantage in some scenarios. You miss things. But for the crowd that values being young and rich, you can't beat it. And that crowd tends to have a lot of disposable income, of course, hmm? On a spacecraft, on the cosmic scale, we think it's going to be pretty useful. So, we do have some good customers. We're doing okay. We think the insurance program will help."

"I guess travel in general?"

"Yeah, it's not the most portable technology, unfortunately. We have plans for a second facility, though—on a great big rock called Novelty Hill on the east side of Lake Washington. We're also planning to build out our main server farm there. It will be a pretty big upgrade.

"There have been discussions of doing really large-scale jumps for ecosystem healing and terraforming, but that's still in the realm of science fiction. We're thinking about it, though.

"There has been some interest from the beauty industry—a lot of interest, actually—and, you know, some interest from the life insurance and investments sectors. We have to be careful of the potential for class warfare types of scenarios. They're a little nervous about that whole thing."

Erich pulled two sets of stapled documents from his top drawer and pushed them across the desk towards Amir and Susan. "Also, the company has a revised contract here for you two that will give you both some additional freedoms. Can you take a look at it and sign it ASAP? That would be great."

Amir scanned the first few paragraphs, then flipped the page and looked over the text there. "You're changing us to contractors, here in section 2B, it says?"

"Yes, the legal department requires that. I really have to

go. They'll tell you all about it in the orientation session on Thursday at 10 a.m.

"You'll notice there's a section there called TravelCare. It's a service offered by all the major jump-point hosts that supplies incoming travelers with various support services. You know, new phones, credit services, financial advice, career and relocation counseling, new vaccines, and so on."

"We're not going to need career counseling if we sign this thing, are we?"

Erich smiled and shook his head.

"The phones thing might be handy," observed Amir.

"Gosh, we just bought top-of-the-line phones when we got here. Wouldn't it make more sense to see if they still work, and just get a new one if we need it?"

"Yeah, I guess so," said Amir.

Susan looked at the Stocks app on her phone. "Wow, Erich, Andna stock is not doing too well these days, is it? Maybe you should make a big jump with us."

"Oh no no no," said Erich as he shook his head. "Those two little jumps—they were enough for the history books. Some bodies have to run this place, hey Li Yan?"

"For sure."

Karl shot an uneasy glance at Susan.

Rössler's phone chimed. He looked at it and walked away.

After he'd left the room, Susan said to Karl, "Are you planning to make a jump, too?"

"Yeah, I'm definitely thinking about it. But I'm not going to jump with you guys right away. Maybe soon, though."

Susan had heard gossip that things were rocky between

him and his wife, but this was the closest to a direct acknowledgement of the situation she'd heard. "Well, I hope it works out," she said.

After a bit of haggling, Susan and Amir finally signed the forms that provided a guarantee of future employment after a jump-time "sabbatical" of 8.17 years. At the 8.17-year mark, there was a good chance some of her coworkers would still be around; at 21 plus, which Susan had been pushing for, not so much. That was the crux of Amir's argument and it was hard to argue with.

So, 8.17 it was. And they would be prepared this time. At the Thursday session, they preregistered for reintegration counseling and TravelCare at a 40 per cent discount.

That Friday, at 3:00 p.m., they were set to depart.

"Hope to see you on the other side," said Susan to Karl and Li Yan. At 2:59 p.m., Amir pulled the door of the transit pod closed and set the "ready" signal.

A moment later, they were gone.

o   o   o

Long Plays

Through the thick glass window of the transit pod, they watched as the light flickered brightly and then went dim. "Whoa, it's pitch-black out there," said Amir. It was so dark the extra-large clock on the far wall—normally the main indicator of transit status—was all but indiscernible in the faint light cast by the tiny status lights on the door panel. Amir unlocked the door of the transit pod, popped it open and listened. It was eerily quiet.

"Hmm. I thought they were supposed to have some sort of welcome program for us?"

"Yeah, me too," said Susan.

They retrieved a pair of flashlights from the supply cabinet inside the pod and stepped onto the platform. Shafts of bright light swept the room as they inspected their surroundings. At least the clock was running.

"There seems to be power."

"Well, it's only 6 a.m.," noted Amir. Maybe it's some sort

of new energy-saving program?" He didn't sound convinced and neither was Susan.

"I dunno. Help me pull this pod off of here."

Amir struggled to tip the pod onto its wheels. "This seems to me like a flaw in the transit pod concept. What if another pod arrives as we are standing here doing this?"

"That would be bad," said Susan, pulling the strap at the top edge of the pod.

"Okay, push!"

In fact, there had been *several* unpleasant incidents with incoming pods, and this had been an area of much research. The establishment of block-out times was not a particularly scalable solution, but it did mitigate the problem. And they could always build more arrival platforms.

It was still dark outside by the time they reached the parking garage and walked toward Susan's parking spot. It was near enough to the exit that they could see the black sky outside as they approached. A driverless van with its lights on cruised slowly down the lane outside the parking garage exit, prowling for a parking spot—or not, thought Susan, as she saw it drive by again a moment later. "Hey, it's still here," she said, pointing to her car with her key fob. Amir walked right past the car, fascinated by something outside.

"Hey, where are you going?"

"Just a moment. This is weird. Come and take a look at this."

The parking lot was much, much smaller than it had been when they left and a new—very tall—building stood right in the middle of the former lot. The lights were on in *that* building.

"New offices, I suppose?"

"Come on, let's get going. I'm hungry."

Amir offered her an energy bar. "I brought a few of these from the pod."

"No thanks. I want *real* food."

She pressed her key fob as they approached her car. "Oh crap, not again." She pushed the button again and again. Nothing.

"You can still unlock it with the key, though, right?" asked Amir.

"Yea, just a minute." She fiddled with her cell phone. "Argh. No signal—again."

"Let me try. Dammit." He pointed his arm in various directions. "No signal? What the hell?"

Susan poked at her phone. No compatible providers. "Dang, I figured we had this one covered."

"There should definitely be signal," Amir insisted.

"Hmm," she said, sliding the phone into her rear pocket. Amir watched her eyes as another van drove slowly by. "Driverless van," she mused. "Two of them! Oh god, no... *three.*" They were circling the lot like sharks.

"I think that one's a delivery van. Prob'ly both. I don't know 'bout the smaller one though."

Susan was not really listening. She was studying the exterior surface of her car—now thick with accumulated dust. "This is different," she mumbled.

"Eww," said Amir as she ran her finger across the filthy

door handle. The unlock button on her key fob did nothing. "Dead battery, as predicted." She opened the door with the key and popped the hatchback. "But this time we're prepared."

Susan opened up the hatchback. "Goddammit. The new battery's been stolen. And the tools, too!"

She lifted the carpet and removed a plastic envelope that said Vehicle QuickStart. She slid out the booklet and opened it. Inside was a bundle of bills in various denominations. "At least the money's still here."

"Looks like we need a jump-start after all, heh?"

A young Asian man came out of the elevator area.

"Hi. Excuse me. We are having some car trouble," said Amir.

He peered at the car with curiosity. "Wow, that's an old gas-mobile, isn't it?"

"Sure is," said Susan, wearing her friendliest smile. "Say, we need a jump start. I've got some jumper cables here. Can you help us?"

"What kind of cables?"

"Jumper cables."

"Sorry, I really don't know how those work."

"I can probably figure it out," said Amir. "Can we take a quick look under your car's hood?"

Under the hood was an electric motor unlike anything Amir or Susan had ever seen.

"Is there a set of, um, low-voltage terminals on there?"

The young man stared blankly as Amir took a photo of his car.

"I'm so sorry. Good luck!"

"Say, before you go, can I ask you a question?"

"Shoot."

"Why is it dark over in the lab?"

"Oh, they pivoted away from that type of research a few years ago into bio-pharm stuff, over here in the new building."

o o o

The first light of dawn was just starting to illuminate some scattered clouds in the eastern sky as the taxi-driver cornered out of the parking lot past two self-driving taxis and out onto the street. Behind them was what looked like another driverless car. The mini mall with the old electronics store was gone. It was now a high-rise, with several new shops on the street level: a hair and nails salon, a sushi restaurant and a bubble tea shop.

Susan directed the driver to stop at the nearest coffee shop. As it turned out, that was an "Artisan Bean" cafe, about ten blocks away. The taxi driver didn't have change, the ten-block trip cost them twenty dollars. The vehicle that had been behind them turned at the next corner and parked. A man and a woman exited the vehicle and walked to the corner.

As Susan and Amir walked down the sidewalk, they noticed the parking meters had no coin slots. It became something of a game: spot the differences.

"Interesting," said Amir. "Look: The license plates are all digital. No keyholes in the door handles. And LED lights everywhere."

Amir looked in the store windows as they passed. Several

were boarded up or plastered with ancient posters. There weren't even any 'For Lease' signs on the derelict storefronts. On the other side of the street, the whole block was fenced off behind a large "Rezoning Proposal" sign. "Uh, business doesn't look that good around here."

"I am not liking the direction this neighborhood has gone in," said Amir.

"Omigod—Orson Bean's Artisan Bean?"

"Who's 'Orson Bean?'" whispered Amir.

"Oh, just about the last person I ever expected to see on a coffee shop sign," said Susan as they approached the side window of the coffee shop. She was increasingly distracted by the view through the window as they approached. "A comedian, uh, mid-20th century," she began.

"Big on a thing called Orgone...." It wasn't clicking with Amir. He shrugged.

Susan tried again. "You never saw that Kate Bush video with the cloudbusting machine? Very cool video. That was about this kooky guy named Wilhelm Reich who claimed to have discovered a biological or cosmic energy he called 'orgone energy.' At the time of his death, he was serving a two-year term for violating the Food and Drug Act by selling and distributing a telephone-booth-size device that supposedly gathered energy from the atmosphere, which he claimed could cure common colds, cancer, and impotence while the patient sat inside. Anyway, this Orson Bean guy was a celebrity and a big believer in all this weird pseudoscience-y Orgone stuff and...." Amir just looked confused.

"Hey," Amir hissed under his breath, tugging at her jacket sleeve. Her last sentence hung there, incomplete, as she noticed what Amir was looking at. The alley at the darkest side of building was lined on both sides by what appeared to be very rough looking homeless people. No, scratch that, realized Amir when he saw the needles.

"Yeesh," said Susan under her breath as they passed.

"Was that a pile of purses in front of that guy?" whispered Amir.

He looked behind them and saw that several of the people were now on their feet and headed toward them.

"Come on." Susan hastened her pace and detoured around the alley toward the lights out front.

"Now that is freakin' scary," he whispered in Susan's direction over the side of his hand, once the junkies were out of earshot.

Things looked a little more promising at the next corner. They could see a bright red open sign on what appeared to be a coffee shop, about a half-block away. They walked past another boarded-up window and a couple of nondescript two-storey office buildings. On the corner of the next block was an inviting-looking café named Coffee and Comforts.

"No shortage of coffee shops, heh?" noted Amir. "That one looks a little better. And it's open."

"Let's get some breakfast here, hey?" he suggested hopefully.

"Yeah, I'm pretty thirsty," he announced as if talking to himself. "Maybe I'll have a juice or something. Apple juice if they've got it."

"Sounds good," said Susan. "One large AJ comin' up."

"It will give us a chance to mingle with the natives," said Amir. "The non-scary ones, at least."

"That's the whole plan," said Susan. "Might be interesting."

When the light changed, a man and a woman crossed the street on the other side as Amir and Susan approached the Coffee and Comforts shop.

Inside the shop, there were several low tables and chairs, and some higher chairs with small tables near the windows. Amir pointed to the one near the end of the counter area. "How 'bout there?"

"Yeah, looks good," said Susan, sizing up the clientele. Across the street, the man and woman watched.

As Amir and Susan walked slowly past the tables inside the coffee shop, everyone was staring at a device of some sort. Some people held phones, others fiddled with watches and glasses. At one table, two teenage girls were playing with what looked like light-up fans. As Susan watched, one powered on her device and opened it up. It displayed—in what appeared to be thin air—an animated multicolor text display that said "Hover-Vu™." The rainbow text dissolved into a rather fancy-looking title page for "Hover-Cats." The device, which was vibrating audibly, then displayed a low-res video of kittens playing. In thin air. A gimmick, sure, but it looked fairly impressive.

"Check that out," said Susan, elbowing Amir. "It seems to be connected to the internet."

"Yeah, I've been watching. It's lots of little LEDs synced to the speed of the motion, I think? Hey, they've got muffins here. Do you want a blueberry muffin?"

"For sure," said Susan. "And a coffee, please. Go ahead and sit down. I'll join you in a minute."

"Hover-Cats, heh?" said Susan as they passed, but the girls seemed oblivious to her as they stared at the glowing gadgets. She persisted. "Could you, ah, tell me where I can buy one of these Hover-Vus?"

One of the girls pulled earbuds out her ears. "You talkin' to us?"

Yes, said Susan. "Where can I buy one of those?"

The other girls—all of whom were wearing earbuds—looked like they were visibly embarrassed even to be seen talking to her. They giggled amongst themselves and whispered to each other as the waitress passed by on her way to take Amir's order. When Susan didn't take the hint and continued to stand there, one said "You don't buy them. They just give 'em away, duh."

"Cool. Thanks for the information."

"Thanks for the information!" "Cool!" they tittered as she walked away, suddenly feeling a little older.

"Did that go well?" asked Amir.

Susan shook her head in mild disbelief. "Omigod. It's like *Idiocracy*[1]," she whispered.

Amir was surreptitiously snapping photos of the other patrons when the beverages and muffins arrived at the table. The girls folded up their Hover-Vu units and slid out of their booth. They put on their backpacks, and headed for the cashier. "Time for school, I guess," said Susan.

"Those are the first teenage girls I've seen in America that weren't carrying cellphones," he whispered.

"There's a couple of guys just sitting over there," whispered Amir. "Maybe one of them has a... oh, wait."

One of the young men tapped the side of his glasses and began laughing to himself. The other was amused by something as well—something different, on some sort of soft-looking tablet.

"See if you can get some information about where to buy a phone," whispered Susan to Amir.

"Hi there," said Amir, trying to sound friendly. "Hey, can you tell me where I can buy one of those...uh, tablets." He pointed to the folding tablet the young man was fixating upon.

Amir spoke a little louder. "Excuse me." Nothing. "Hello?"

The young man finally noticed him and pulled a wireless earbud out of his ear.

[1] 2006 American science fiction comedy film in which a man wakes up from 500 years of hibernation and realizes that he is the smartest man on the planet.

"What...?"

"Sorry to bother you but we're not from around here. Where can we buy a tablet like yours?"

"Tablet? You mean my phone? I dunno, man. I don't think they sell them. They just give 'em to you when you sign up."

"And where can we sign up?"

"Lots of places." He pointed to the street, plugging his earbud back in.

"There's Banter," said his friend, who seemed a little less out of it.

"Um, oh yeah, Banter. Yeah, right across the street. They're okay."

"My sister has one," said his friend. "They're a bit banky, but they're okay."

"Yeah, we don't want 'em too banky," said Amir, shooting a confused look toward Susan. "Thanks guys."

But the friends were already focused back on their devices, and didn't respond.

"It's a bit creepy, isn't it? What's '*banky*?'" whispered Amir.

Susan shrugged and finished off her cup of exceptionally potent dark-roasted coffee. "Expensive, maybe?"

Susan ate the last bite of her muffin and looked at the clock on the wall. "Hey, it's almost eight-thirty. We should find out what time that Banter place opens," she said to Amir.

He downed a half-glass of apple juice in a single gulp and pulled the last piece of his muffin from its paper liner. "Sure, let's go."

After, Susan and Amir paid the bill using one of the hundred-dollar bills. Although the cashier had eyed the money suspiciously, she accepted it without a fuss, and gave them back five polymer bills and two large coins. Behind her, the prices on the racks of muffins and pastries changed as the clock marked 8:30.

"Oh, may I have a receipt, please?"

"Are you paying with phone or card?"

"Paper's fine."

"Paper? We don't do paper."

"22 bucks. That's not bad, I guess."

"May I see?"

She handed the bill to Amir.

"Whoa, look at the tax!"

"I'm a little surprised that we didn't have to pay until *after* the meal," said Amir. "Almost every coffee shop I've ever been to in America makes you pay when you order."

"That's true," agreed Susan. "But when I was a kid it didn't used to be like that around here. I wonder if they've found that people are more likely to add on to their order—you know, pay for a refill or have dessert or that sort of thing—if they only have to go through the purchase procedure once?"

In fact, the whole marketing campaign behind Artisan Bean's was that it was a good old-fashioned coffee shop. Its success had led to a host of competitors, including Coffee and Comforts. Better coffee, better couches.

o o o

Despite the time, they were surprised to find that the door of the BANTR store was already unlocked. Amir poked his head inside, looking for a salesperson. "Hello? Anybody here?"

"Welcome to BANTR," said a voice coming from a panel just inside the door. "Scan a code for more information about any of our products or services. Or ask me a question. Have a great day!"

"Is there a sales clerk here?"

"I can help you complete any sales transaction or service upgrade you may require. Just ask!" said the bot cheerfully.

"Well, we already have phones. But we want to get service. Can we do that here?"

"I get it. You want BANTR service for your phone. No problem! Just select your device from the list to see your Easy-Vu Upgrade options."

Susan looked for her phone's name in the list. It wasn't there. She selected "Unknown phone."

"I'm sorry, your [unknown] device is too old for the all-new suite of BANTR services. You can trade in your device using our Easy-Vu video kiosk. Would you like to do that?"

"Sure."

"Your device is worth $0. Would you like to recycle it now?"

"I'm so glad we paid extra for these state-of-the-art phones," said Susan.

"Heh, 10G," marveled Amir as he looked at the large picture in the window. He noticed the woman and her companion across the street.

"Welcome to Easy-Vu. Are your devices already using BANTR services? Say 'yes,' 'no,' or 'I don't know.'"

"No. Is there a person I can speak to?"

The machine seemed to pretend it didn't hear the question.

"Wow, you're in luck. We've got a special discount for you when you switch to BANTR services. Would you like more information?"

"This sucks."

"It sounds like you're not happy with your current service. Say 'I want more' for more choices from BANTR."

"Let's go."

"Look at this," said Amir. He had a camera app running on one of the demo tablet-phones. He pointed it at the window facing the street and tapped on the image. The camera zoomed in on the woman and her companion across the street. As the image zoomed in, it brightened and sharpened the image. It was the fake doctors.

Amir feigned a cough. "I think we're being followed...."

o o o

10

All the Rage

When Erich and Li Yan arrived for the usual 9:00 meeting, Susan and Amir were already there, standing at the back of the room. Amir was surprised at how much older Erich looked than he did in the family photos on his desk. Li Yan had a new tattoo and a better haircut.

Li Yan threw her arms around Susan. "Omigod. It's great to see you. It's been so long!"

She turned to Amir and put her hands on his shoulders. "And you, oh my goodness, you are a sight for sore eyes."

"It's great to see you Amir," said Erich. "It seems like only last week to you, I guess?"

"That's no exaggeration, said Amir.

"Nice hairdo, Li Yan," remarked Susan.

"Thanks. Wow, you haven't aged a day. Must be nice."

"Well, did you see anything interesting on your travels today?" asked Erich.

"Well, I was seriously unnerved by how subservient the

people we saw were to their devices, like those fold-up Hover-Vu gizmos."

"Yeah, those things are all the rage these days."

"What I want to know is what the hell happened to the reintegration services that were supposed to get? We paid for those services, so…how do we get them?"

"Yeah, that program was very expensive to maintain and was discontinued a couple of years ago, unfortunately. I can get you a refund for that if you have the receipt."

"A *receipt*? Seriously? Never mind. Look, I've been thinking. I'd like to work as kind of a project historian. I feel it is our scientific duty to capture an accurate record of the dates, events and people for historical purposes. And possibly a documentary."

"However, there are a few things we need. Most importantly, we need a company credit card and a supporting line of credit to be maintained in perpetuity, so that we can buy or rent essential items as we move forward. If we're going to be your pioneers, we need these basic provisions."

"Secondly, we need to know that the company is committed to maintaining the infrastructure and equipment related to this project, insofar as these commitments are compatible with the current and future goals of the project."

"Can we stop there for a moment?" Rössler sat down in the chair at the end of the table. He motioned to Amir and Susan to sit down.

"I understand your concerns—I really do—but there are a few things you need to know."

"First, I'm sorry this wasn't made clear to you yesterday,

but the research continued after you made that first five-year jump. We had other volunteers—quite a few, in fact—go through the time gate, as we now call it. So, you show up and jump again, a further eight years. At this point, there have been over a hundred—closer to two hundred, actually—people jump forward. More than half of them volunteered before you took that second big jump. Most of them jumped smaller amounts. In young people, we saw a spike before age 21. Quite a few young women said they would like to just skip the years 19 to 22 completely—and asked us if we could make it work that way instead. We didn't interview kids, but I can tell you that if you interviewed my kids, they would definitely want to skip that week leading up to Christmas—or Spring Break, hey? Ha ha."

"The people we surveyed in their fifties, some of them said they just want to skip to the retirement pension immediately. Several women said they would skip nine months to have an easier pregnancy. Heh! That's not the way that works, but it's an interesting data point."

"There are seasonal bumps here and there. Several of those surveyed said they would only skip weekdays. Dec 29 is not so popular. Anything over a few months starts to impact your employability, so that's a real risk we want to be careful about. I mean where are truck drivers today, right?"

"The speculative investors make their long-term bets. Then they don't have to wait around as long to reap the rewards. The investments don't always pay off, of course. But the long plays can pay very well."

"The ability to essentially disappear from history for a

number of years, well that's been attractive to some of the criminals out there, of course. There are quite a few plausible scenarios that people have expressed interest in."

In fact, there was a thriving underground scene among Hollywood stars and other well-heeled celebrities who managed to stretch their fifteen minutes of fame out across several decades, with the help of black-market jump brokers who arranged to get them fake IDs and transit passes.

There was also a booming business in "cool-off consultants," who specialized in long-term damage control. They helped fading stars take advantage of future nostalgia waves and rekindled careers of celebrities who had managed to disgrace themselves one way or another on social media. These consultants helped coordinate re-releases of the erstwhile stars' best productions and best-loved media memories while re-introducing them to an audience primed for their brand of "new nostalgia."

Indeed, there were consultancy businesses serving—or exploiting, depending on your point of view—virtually every subgroup of the time-jumping population. The fact was, people became less employable, the longer they were out of the workforce. So, retraining and job placement services were essential.

A common tactic was to purchase bonds, property, rare vehicles, artworks, and so on likely to increase in value over time and then jump forward to collect on the accrued value.

When Susan shared her frustration over the cancellation of the reintegration program, Li Yan explained that things weren't quite as bleak as Erich had made them out to be.

There were, she explained, third-party contractors offering programs to help move people into areas where their job skills were likely to be more valuable. 'Retro-modern Aestheticians,' for example, were apparently in big demand.

"GP-type doctors, on the other hand, were much more valuable in the *last* couple of decades than we expect they will be in the next few," explained Li Yan. "And there's not much demand for retail clerks, eh? Ha ha. Or the taxi driver business. Maybe that's a good thing."

"It's a bit funny, I think," said Erich. "The automation industry has focused its efforts on reducing the drudgery in many of the jobs near the bottom of the list of careers ranked by complexity. Meanwhile modern AI-driven automation has devastated huge swathes of highly skilled disciplines, replacing the jobs of financial planners and bankers and supervisors who just don't perform at their pay scale as well as the machines. They are more at risk of joblessness than the ones near the bottom of the list."

"You saw what happened when we set up those counseling services for time jumpers. The program didn't scale well. You, Susan, as a mathematician, must know better than most people that skills that were valuable in the past aren't as valuable in the future. We have machines that are amazing at advanced mathematics—far beyond any human in terms of computational power. Already, we're seeing very progressive results from our mathematical systems. We really don't see much of a future for your skill-set. All our analytics are automated already."

"Oh, for god's sake. I'm not even going to begin to argue

the value of a human mathematician. Fine. I'll go forward then. What's the largest jump anyone has done to date?"

"Actually, your 8.17-year jump was one of the largest during that entire period. There have, however, been a few other big jumps—reckless ones, in some cases. We had a couple of people tell us they were committed to making multiple jumps. So, 406 years is the largest cumulative jump itinerary we've seen to date."

"Wow."

"We have no idea whether they actually completed all those jumps, and have no idea how they're doing, of course."

"The good news is the board has continued to support the idea of employee pensions based on years of service in the company, even if you've skipped ahead. So, at 22 years old, plus 5.05 years in your first big jump, and now 8.17 years in the most recent one, you have accumulated the retirement pension-eligible work time credit equivalent to that of a 35-year-old employee. So, only 30 years to go, and you're eligible."

"The trend in jumping these days is in the opposite direction. Shorter jumps are on the increase—strategic jumps designed to minimize risks and maximize benefits."

"Aha," said Amir. "That's important to study—to understand."

"However, we have done tests of numerous subjects, where we have imposed hundreds of smaller time-jumps, allowing us to study various medical and psychological results. All of which we consider valuable, of course."

"We have also set up a program we call jump-trackers, so

that you can find other jumpers, and other jumpers can find you. It's part of the profile kept for each participant in the program."

"You must have a profile for me—and one for Amir, right?"

Rössler nodded.

Amir shot a glance at Susan, suddenly worried that she was about to accuse Rössler of having his people spying on them on the street.

"Okay, tell us what your career viability estimator suggests as the best possible times for us to jump to."

"It's not quite that simple," said Rössler. "It's a big world, with lots of economic, cultural and societal differentiators. The Middle East is still, you know, volatile. It has been so for a great many years, and we just don't see that changing much in the foreseeable future. So, people in areas like that, they have different needs. Amir probably knows that Mumbai continues to be a place where mathematicians are very highly valued. So, you might find that this would be a good place for you to go. Wall Street, not so much."

"Our system places you in Mumbai, India or São Paulo, Brazil for best economic results. Of course, you may not actually have to be there—you can simply telework into those areas for many positions."

"There are other possibilities, of course. Australia, Canada, and a few others, are still hiring from outside the country, particularly in the biotech-math crossover markets. I've got a report here for each of you. It lists the geographical areas on a timeline with, you know, a kind of a best-guess estimate for which place and which time might be best for each of you. It also lists some suggested courses you might wish to take to bring your skills up to meet the most common current employment requirements. You know, the tools and the latest programs and all that stuff."

"Any questions about that?"

Susan was temporarily speechless, so utterly outraged she was at what she was hearing. Amir shook his head. Mumbai didn't sound *too* bad as a possible career move.

"I'm sure you'll probably have some after you read these reports. I've sent them to you now. If you would be good enough to review these documents, you can schedule an appointment with me and we will see what can do to get you fixed up with a future that really works in your favor."

Erich looked at the clock on the wall. "It's, ah, ten to ten and you guys have to get down to the big hall for the 10 a.m. briefing session there, so we should wrap this up now. See you here tomorrow, same time, okay?"

"I'm sorry, that's really *not* okay," said Susan, much to Amir's surprise. "First of all," she said, "where's Karl?"

"Karl was laid off, I'm afraid. The AI does all our programming now."

"And what assurance do we have that we won't be laid off, as well?"

"I'm sorry to say we don't actually have positions open *here* for you guys, either. You'll be transferred to one of the recommended placement locations, or you can accept the termination-of-contract settlement offer I have here."

"Oh dear," said Amir.

Susan's frustration boiled over. "I'm done here. This is bullshit. You discontinued your last support service, and now you're telling me about this new jump-tracking program, which I fully expect will be discontinued just like the last one was. Just send me forward. You can stay if you want Amir, but I'm out. And Dr. Rössler: you and your fake doctors—those spies we saw following us—you can all go to hell."

Erich's temper flared. "You are now in violation of your NDA, young lady," he said, threateningly.

Li Yan looked acutely embarrassed.

"Oh my god, you're so arrogant," said Susan, her rage suddenly melting into regret. "I really don't want to fight," she said quietly. "I just want to go forward. When can I make a jump?"

"Ah, there's a new Government Service Fee. It has to be paid before exit visas are granted."

"I really don't care. I've got the money from my mom's apartment and my investments."

He handed her a tablet with the details.

"Holy crap! $180,000 per person?" She handed the tablet back to Erich. "Fine, whatever. Can I go now? Just tell me where to pay and dial me up a Fibonacci index of 43."

"Good god, Susan, that's a huge jump."

"Yes, I know. 237.12 years, roughly."

"That's really not recommended. It could be a death sentence—some catastrophic ecological collapse. Or nuclear winter, or a pandemic, or some such thing—it's really very dangerous, what you're proposing."

"Oh, come on," she argued. "It could just as well be a new

renaissance age of math and science! To me, it's like traveling to some other planet. You might die, but the chance to set foot on an entirely new world is a very attractive proposition. And for the first time, we've really got something here that can help us get there." Her mood softened a bit and she shook her head. "There's nothing for me here."

"You realize the chances of there being a working accelerator on the other end are close to zero, right?" said Li Yan. "Very close. We don't even run the probabilities that far, there's just no chance."

"I'm kind of counting on that, to be honest with you. The future's not what I thought it would be. And humankind's worst tendencies seem to be getting worse, not better."

"You might be suffering from post-traumatic stress disorder, Susan," said Erich. "There are people that can help you if you're depressed."

"I'm sure there's an app for that," snapped Susan.

"That's not very funny," said Amir.

"I'm not fucking depressed," she argued. "It's just that this environment of quarterly profit-and-loss corporate *bullshit* is not the environment in which I want to live. I'd like to know if extinction is humanity's destiny, or whether we, as a species, will get past our greedy and warring ways. I feel certain that we will. We *have* to."

"The way I figure it," she said, "the farther ahead we go, the greater the likelihood that there will be other working time travel machines at the other end to continue the journey forward or perhaps even go back again. I figure that if we haven't figured out how to go back in time by then, we probably never will. I also have a bit of a fond spot for the period in human history roughly 4500 years ago, when the pyramids were being built, so that's a motivating factor for me to want to go back there, as well. I've always wanted that."

"It was probably not great in terms of working conditions, though," joked Li Yan.

Susan wouldn't take the bait. "It's partly based on risk factor analysis, and that's good enough for me. I already know there's nothing here for me."

"And what about you, Amir?"

"I'm afraid I'm not that brave," admitted Amir. "I was thinking of traveling forward to one or more of those meeting points in the next 10 to 15 years. Honestly, I just want to meet some more open-minded people, to see how we as a species will deal with things like climate change and, you know, see how things will progress across one's lifespan. We're very hung up as a society these days—so much prejudice. I think people are probably going to be cooler in the future."

Rössler nodded. "Well, it's certainly part of our mandate to meet other people, share information, and take the steps that enable us to move forward more confidently as a group— as a team."

He gestured, as he often did, with a wave of his hand. "We set up this program to allow forwarders to share knowledge to mitigate the risks they face, such as potential critical resource depletion, extinctions in the food chain, potential societal upheavals, banking system collapse, large-scale terrorist attack, catastrophic ecosystem disruption, global pandemic, or even global nuclear war." He punctuated each disastrous bullet-point with a jab of his hand.

"On the bright side," added Amir, "I think I must have a lot of money accruing in my long-term bonds and investment accounts."

"You should check that," said Li Yan. "After news of the program was leaked to the public, the government enacted some very discriminatory laws targeting 'time migrants.' Ugh, I hate that term. It's like the 2020s all over again."

"There's one thing I think Susan and I have learned from our travels so far," said Amir. "The more you travel, the easier it is to see what's really going on. I think we've become a little wiser, or at least a little more interested in sharing information."

"And that's an argument against long jumps right there," observed Erich. "And believe me, he said, if you ever settle down and start a family, you won't want to miss a minute of it."

"Look," he said, "why don't you and Susan explore some of the other jump-stations we've built around the country? There's the one in Houston, one in Redmond, and one planned for the Chicago area. We can supply you with the exit visas. But you'll have to cover your own plane fares."

"We could drive," suggested Amir.

"All the way to Redmond?" said Susan, incredulously. "I'm not sure my Camry would make it."

"It only takes a few days. We could rent a car. One with air conditioning."

Susan didn't say anything, but it looked like she was at least *considering* the idea.

"Looking at this as a math problem," said Li Yan, "we know the number of people and exactly which time-periods they passed through on their way to any given point. Thus, we can construct a knowledge graph as a density map. There's a high probability that the time periods and geographic areas with the most coverage will provide better predictive results."

Amir nodded in agreement. "It's a compelling argument, to at least give the idea of data-driven predictions based on multiple jumps a try. As a mathematician, Susan, I'm sure you can see the logic in that."

Susan nodded.

"After all," continued Li Yan, "you get one chance at passing by each time period. It's probably best to pick and choose carefully, using the data set to help inform future predictions and choices."

"All right. You've convinced me," admitted Susan. "They must have a list like that for their briefing sessions. Are you ready to sit through another one of those, Amir?"

Amir shrugged. It was better that than staying here with Rössler. And it felt brave.

o o o

It made sense to head to Redmond first. It was far too hot in Houston at this time of year. They decided they would maximize the variety of experiences by comparing several short-term jumps and subsequent briefing sessions at each of the available jump-stations. To add value to the briefing session experiences, Susan planned to interview both incoming and outgoing jumpers. Now that there was a hefty fee involved, she expected a different demographic for outgoing jumpers.

After all the talk about renting a new car for the trip, Susan had her old car tuned up and the tires checked. She decided it was in good enough shape to make the trip to Redmond. And, at least on the interstate, there were still enough gas stations to get there.

"You'll be the camera operator, okay?" she said as she buckled herself into the driver's seat. Sounds good to me, said Amir as she pulled out of the parking lot and pressed the mileage counter reset button. They were off on their big road trip.

o o o

Amir opened the door of a washroom at a diner in Fergus Falls to find Susan kissing a random guy in the hall outside. "Bye," she said as he entered the washroom.

"He was just waiting and we got talking," she said nonchalantly.

"That has *never* happened to me," said Amir.

The sun was just coming up when they reached Fall City. "We're close now," said Amir, looking at the GPS. "We're only about twenty minutes away. Do you want to stop for breakfast?"

"Nah, let's find the place first and then we'll eat," said Susan as she changed lanes.

When they reached the facility, they showed their badges

and found out from the clerk at the information desk that the next arrival was scheduled for 9 a.m. A manager came by and very graciously set them up in a small room near the briefing center where they could record their interviewees.

Susan captured as many data points as she could. She recorded the numbers of incoming and outgoing travelers, their age, sex, marital status, work history and any other information they were willing to share. There were three briefing sessions that day and they attended them all. Amir recorded brief videos of every interviewee and they chose a few people to feature in longer video segments. The data revealed some interesting trends.

They learned that as the frequency of flash-forwarders increased, the number of those who fell into refugee status increased. Most of the people who jumped were out of work and/or recently separated. Many had some sort of medical condition. And almost all the ones who didn't fall into one of these groups had a financial reason for making the jump —many of which sounded suspiciously like get-rich-quick schemes to Amir.

Briefing sessions shifted from their early emphasis on money-making strategies and long-term financial planning to an increasingly common refrain: loopholes exploited by previously lucrative disruption strategies were closing faster, recommended jump-distances were getting shorter, and crowds at the briefing sessions were getting bigger.

And the type of person who was showing up at the sessions seemed to be changing, too. Adventurers were becoming homeless refugees.

Groups arriving from earlier periods tended to find the treatment they received from various government departments unacceptable. They were refugees without hope of return, burdened by an inability to function properly in an environment that became increasingly alien and disruptive the farther forward they jumped. At a certain point, no one wanted them. Plans to build a jump station in Chicago were canceled.

There were other controversies, too. Unscrupulous executives at the Andna jump station in Redmond, Washington were convicted of money-laundering when, in a classic example of unfortunate timing, the evidence appeared during the lengthy trial.

There were also allegations of kidnapping and murder, although these were never proven, as the bodies were never found.

Sure, company officials tried to spin the news into more positive territory with stats about maturing biotech markets and long-term investments in climate change opportunities in the Pacific Northwest, but it didn't convince Andna investors. After the briefing, the company's stock hit a historic low.

After the final Redmond briefing session, Susan and Amir walked silently to the elevator. Amir pressed L and, a moment later, the elevator doors opened.

At dinner that evening, Amir ran their profiles through the WhenAdvisor app. He held the screen up and flattened it out for Susan to see. She finished her mouthful. "13.21 years, huh? Let's take it."

○ ○ ○

11

Archives and Agendas

_"Spacetime points only acquire their physical sig-
nificance because matter is moving through them."_
—STANFORD ENCYCLOPEDIA OF PHILOSOPHY

Unfortunately, there was no 13.21-year briefing session. Instead, they arrived to a bombed-out building, with only a reconstructed arrival deck and some crudely-lit defense department signage. The elevator down to P1 was out of service and the stairwell door was locked. An arrow on a barrier with flashing yellow lights said EXIT THIS WAY. Most of the other areas were dark, the doors locked.

They followed the signs to the exit. A high fence surrounded the building. There was, however, a second building nearby. The glass doors parted as they approached. A woman sat at the security desk.

"We had a car parked over in that building on the P1 level. Do you know how we can get to it?"

She scanned their jump-visa badges. "You say it was on P1? One moment, please." She looked at their ID record. "Sorry, those vehicles have all been removed. The underground parking garage completely collapsed and most of the vehicles down there were complete write-offs. All unclaimed vehicles were recycled or sold as scrap."

"So much for your car."

"Well, it was getting pretty hard to find gas stations, anyway. Come on, let's see if the hotel is still there."

o o o

Archived newscasts revealed that Andna had entered into bankruptcy and had been bailed out by the government, with a new pro-military mandate.

The reports said Andna had recently ousted former CEO Isaac Stern when the company became a decentralized autonomous organization using mini-blockchain technologies.

There were also stories of anti-refugee hostilities and outright terrorism. Someone hacked a self-driving van owned by Isaac Stern himself (!) to drive through the front window of the Princeton Research Center. And then on July 2, someone at the Redmond facility pushed a bomb-laden transit pod two days into the future. According to reports, the Redmond accelerator complex was heavily damaged when a transit pod containing multiple explosive devices went off inside the accelerator chamber itself. Official information was vague, but the media was saying the bombing had been in response to the "No more refugees" note found earlier that week inside the crashed self-driving van at the company's headquarters in

Trenton, New Jersey. Others saw it as a response to an initiative to ban human-driven vehicles as a way of reducing road fatalities. Critics had argued that self-driving vehicles should be banned instead, due to the spike in such vehicles being used as bomb carriers and other terrorist agenda items.

"We'll have to find a functioning time-gate if we want to do any more jumping."

"Houston is the closest."

"It's not that close. It's more than 2300 miles. It's 2800 to Trenton."

"Well, I guess Houston it is. I think we should investigate that and, if the project is still active, go there."

"Wow," said Amir, doomscrolling through an article about climate change. "Galveston is pretty much gone. And look at this picture of Seaside Heights." He thought for a moment. "Before we go, what do you say we contact a few of these journalists that have written about the rise and fall of Andna and see if they are interested in our story. I really think they might be. And the story deserves to be told."

"But Amir," Susan protested, "that would be a direct violation of our NDA."

"Which was with a corporation that no longer exists, I remind you."

"Well, I *would* like to document this properly—and then we can go, okay?"

"Ohh, ho ho," Amir chuckled, looking through the bankruptcy proceedings. "I'm not sure if I should even tell you about this."

"Takes a lot to surprise me these days, Amir. Let's hear it."

"Okay. Your professor was named Rutherford, wasn't he? Richard Rutherford?" Susan nodded.

"It says here he was a silent partner at MPAX, which became Andna. And now he's filed a claim against the company."

"For some reason, that neither surprises nor amuses me. But, yeah, I can believe it."

He warned me about something like this, she thought to herself.

Amir looked up from his Foldex and smiled broadly. "Aha. This is great news. There *has* been a new test facility built in Houston, at the Nasa Space Center. They developed a version intended to fit into an interstellar spacecraft."

"Must be a very small one."

"Well, apparently it is big enough to work. It says here that it was designed by none other than the team that developed the MPAS tech. That would probably include Li Yan and Karl."

Susan's mood brightened noticeably. "Yes!"

"And probably George's code, too."

Amir swiped at the screen and continued reading. "Hmm, I dunno. The article only mentions Dr. Rössler. Whatever, it's still worth getting in touch."

"Anyway, listen to this: the design is optimized for producing a short-range Alcubierre field effect. And supposedly it works."

"Fantastic. Is there any contact information supplied?"

"No, not really. It just says that the Nasa experiment is located in a new facility in Houston."

"Hmm. Maybe they've relocated to Houston?"

"Yep, that sounds about right. I'll track the office number down."

o o o

Several phone calls later...

"It's a closed project, and there's no one there that we know, or that knows us, for that matter," said Amir. "So much for making history."

Susan shrugged. "Ehh, I was never doing this for the fame. It took 358 years for mathematicians to prove Fermat's last theorem. The fact that Wiles[2] eventually cracked the problem —just a few years before I was born—that's worth living 358 years for, right there. Great breakthroughs take time."

"Aha!" said Amir. "It says here that, in addition to the NASA research facility, there's also an Andna office and briefing center in Houston, in an area called Skyscraper Shadows, just south of the Hobby airport. So, there's still a chance."

"Hello. Have I reached the Andna office in Houston, Texas? Yes, thank you."

"I'm calling for Dr, Rössler. Yes. Yes, I'll hold. Thank you."

"Hello, I'm holding for Dr. Rössler. What? *You're* Dr. Rössler?"

---

[2] British mathematician Andrew Wiles

On the other end of the phone, a young blonde woman sat at a desk on the third floor. On it was a metal plaque that said Erica Rössler. "You were looking for my father?"

"Yes, has he retired?"

"No, I'm sorry to say he died a little more than five years ago."

"I'm very sorry to hear that."

"You said your name was Roy."

"Yes. Amir Roy."

"Ah, *mister* Roy! You must know Susan Everett?"

"Yes, she's.... We're planning to be in your area soon. Yes, later this week. Friday? Yes, that sounds good. See you then." He signaled 'thumbs up' to Susan.

"Transit options from here to Houston," said Amir to the Foldex.

"Hmm, okay," he said, examining the options. "There are a few ways to get there. The bus options are fairly brutal, though. It's two-and-a-half days by bus, 36 hours by car, or about four hours by air. Maybe we should rent a car?"

"Might be handy. Can you get us one?"

"Oh yeah, I'll get a self-driving one. We can sleep on the way."

o o o

When Susan and Amir arrived at Skyscraper Shadows, they were surprised and delighted to find Karl there. He had aged visibly, but immediately smiled at the first sight of them.

"Hey," exclaimed Karl as he approached, "Look who came to take me out to lunch." After an uncharacteristically warm embrace from the usually reserved Austrian, Karl gestured to the control room where several other workers in Andna lab coats sat at various workstations. "Ya, I'm a contractor now." He lowered his voice and nodded toward the door. "Come on, I'll show you around."

When they were outside the room, he spoke quietly. "It's okay, you know. The benefits aren't as good, but we don't have to suffer through those crazy mid-year reviews."

"Hey, how come your badge and the sign and everything still says Andna? I thought the company was in bankruptcy."

"Not exactly," replied Karl. "The military bailed us out. So it's a different legal entity—Andna LLC—now."

He gestured toward the main hall. "Come on," he said, "there are no cameras in the kitchen."

He opened the cooler and retrieved a can of grapefruit soda. "Go ahead, they don't mind. You're a guest." He popped the lid and took a sip. "You know, just before I was let go, I was working on developing a system for quantum communications between wave-station facilities."

"Was that the 'quantum chain' idea we used to talk about?" asked Susan.

"Ya, basically," smiled Karl, running his finger around the rim of the can. "It didn't work very well for a long time. I eventually realized it didn't really need to work perfectly."

Karl smiled. "When Erich Rössler died, they released his notes. He never jumped again after that first little one, after all that. He always talked about it, but he never did. More of a family man, I guess. But Li Yan went and then I did, after my divorce."

"I'm sorry to hear that."

"Nah, it's fine. My kids are both in their twenties now, and they still live with my ex-wife, so I think I got a bit lucky, really."

"But, yeah, Li Yan and I—we'd agreed beforehand to meet here. Er, now, I should say—you know what I mean."

What Karl *didn't* mention was that his relationship with Li Yan was the reason for his divorce.

○ ○ ○

Novelty

It had been a beautiful October night. Karl and Li Yan were on their way to the Pacific Northwest to review progress on the new Novelty Hill facility. They had chosen the relative luxury and expansive legroom of an autonomous taxi versus taking a train or an airplane. Unlike either of those options, the taxi was completely private and allowed them to relax and even sleep on the way there. Or drink. And, as is so often the case with alcohol, a few too many drinks led to a night of errant judgment and an unplanned tryst, interrupted only by an unexpected video call from Mrs. Schraeder. In a more sober state, they might have looked and sounded more innocent, but the video stream showed Karl's wife all she needed to see.

Karl thought about that trip for a moment and then managed a slightly sad smile in Susan's direction. "Hey, you'll like this. I came up with this idea of how to synchronize and propagate waves between facilities and I got them to hire me back as a contractor to lead a team to develop it. Cool, right?"

He slid a pop can across the table in front of him. "We'd get two accelerator stations going; they'd generate the waves. Then, station number two would replicate and propagate the wave signature from number one. We'd be able to then position the effect anywhere along that path—with the idea that it would speed up spacecraft or interplanetary communications."

"It certainly would."

"It did," added Karl.

"Yeah, well, our mandate was to come up with a compelling value prop. Stern was pretty desperate to get additional funding by year three." He lowered his voice. "Good riddance to that fucking guy," he said quietly.

"And now...?"

"It is interesting, he mused, "watching how the demographic for the jumpers has changed over time. I honestly thought there'd be more researchers—you know, more academics. But it's almost all older people. Not like you guys. God, you're still so young."

His phone chirped. "Just a sec. We've got an incoming jump. Ah, watch! This is from 10 seconds ago."

On the deployment platform monitor screen, a group flashed into view. "See? So many old people."

"So, are these just civilians—you know, paying customers?"

"Officially, no, but there have been a few—what shall I call them? —*mysteries*. We were told everything done on the time-shifting project was kept top secret at Andna and then, when the military took it over, the emphasis shifted to strategic stuff, like ghosting, where agents jump in and jump out with sensitive information—that sort of thing. We hardly ever see military activity here, so I'm pretty sure they have their own top-secret facilities."

"So, I'm curious," said Amir. "If this thing is so top-secret, how come there are Wikipedia pages about it?"

"There's apparently a new org inside NASA known as ASTRA, the Aeronautics and Space-Time Research Administration. We should definitely contact these guys."

"Definitely," agreed Karl.

Amir was head-down in the Foldex again. "Hmm, it says here that the pioneering research done by the MPAS team was the catalyst for what—just a couple of years ago—became the biggest innovation in warp field transaction technologies: the ability to entangle a checksum bit with the source, then set the bit upon arrival at the temporal destination point."

"Ya, and as it turned out, that proved to be *very* useful. Let me show you."

He showed them a NASA presentation detailing their new ASTRA division's temporal and aerospatial focus and the related strategic goals and objectives.

"Wow," marveled Amir. "That's our tech."

"Ya, inner *and* outer space," mused Karl.

"By the way, where's Li Yan these days?"

"She's around. She works upstairs these days managing the dev department. Funny, isn't it—how people who love what they do tend to get promoted into positions where they are not doing the thing they loved the most."

"Oh, I guess that's not fair. She's a great manager, and I'm sure she's making way more money than me at this point."

"Let me see if I can reach her." He dialed her on the desk phone and threw her video feed up on the big screen.

"Hi Karl. What's up?"

"Hey, look who's here."

"Omigosh. Wow. Look at you two rock stars. I'll come down. See you in a minute."

When Li Yan arrived, she gave them both big hugs. "You know I just celebrated my 46th birthday," she said.

"Hey, congratulations."

"Ya, Happy birthday."

"Have either of you even celebrated one since we first met?"

"Oh, I dunno. I sort of stopped counting the years at least."

"Hey, we heard about the NASA thing over at the Space Center. Do you think there might be any positions available either there or here for people like us? I thought maybe you or Karl might know someone."

"Unfortunately, there aren't any jobs here," said Li Yan. "Matter of fact, this whole place is closing down. It's the weather. The facility has flooded twice in the last five years, and the hurricanes have been really brutal over the last couple of years. Karl's team is moving back to Trenton and, well, I'm not sure what I'm going to do."

She pulled her hair behind her ear. "But yeah, I can hook you up with someone at NASA. The NASA team moves way slower than we ever did, though. Although they're essentially continuing the work that we pioneered, they seem to be more interested in delivering and marketing new time-shift services than partnering on research projects."

"To be fair, though," said Karl, "we have to give them credit for at least one great innovation: ASTRA scientists discovered that the "ring of light" phenomenon we had observed and documented provided the opportunity to send a few qubits worth of data. Not much, but enough to send a brief status signal: ok, blocked, toxic, etc."

"Do tell."

"This is done using a special type of measurement-based quantum computing they call the cluster state, in which more than two particle-states become entangled."

"By sending one particle forward, and validating the other against a measured source, the multipartite entanglement can be used for space-time communications—rather poorly, I might add, due to a phenomenon called monogamy of entanglement, in which the total wavefunction can't be written as a product of single-particle wavefunctions. But they were still able to use it to pass crude messages via state estimation. So that's very cool, and very useful."

"Wait, I'm confused," confessed Susan. "How would this communications system even work?"

"Well," said Karl, drawing a series of concentric circles. "George and I were kinda brainstorming one day, thinking along the lines of an audio wave as an admittedly simplistic analogy for our quantum wave." He drew a pair of small circles on opposite sides of the rings. "Kinda like you did that time with your record player analogy, remember?"

"Yeah, that was a good day."

"Well, this is nothing like that," Karl teased.

Karl added a third circle to the drawing and drew a triangle between the points. "Anyway, when we added a third point, we got a mappable planar space and we actually had a few successful tests." He drew an imaginary dot in midair above the surface. "The plan was to have four, to get a full 3D coordinate system. We were pissing around thinking about coordinate systems and they managed to get a full-on communications system working."

"They really beat us to the punch on that one. Fortunately, they shared their implementation with us."

"That's one of the *only* things they've shared with us, mind you."

Karl retraced the key ideas with his pen as he described them in detail. "Like us, they started with the idea of a mono waveform, where the same wave is being amplified across two channels, which you might think of as 'left' and 'right.' We thought, 'why not manipulate the *balance* to change the relative amplitude of the modulation channels, the same way one might experience a change in the spatial position of an audio image as it moves between the left and right channels?'"

"Of course," added Li Yan, "the quantum equivalent is a little different, so we eventually figured out how to generate a resonant wave and derive an entangled set of wavefunctions, to avoid the inability to duplicate the original values, see?"

"Wow, yeah."

"Heh. And we kinda got bogged down there for a while. It took us *ages* to get that working."

"At that point, we were focused on separating the

spin-entangled electron pairs. This way, the multidimensional waveset could be manipulated along the available axes: for example, along a straight line for a 'stereo pair' of wavefunction values, or with additional control points for a fully multi-dimensional temporal wave-space."

"Interesting. Quantum wave-space in this case, of course."

"You betcha. We knew that when we ran though the Hilbert space routines on the accelerator—those were the ones you came up with, of course—we were essentially flattening out 3D space-time with a Schrödinger equation. And when we flatten out that toroidal warp ring we are generating, the distance time's arrow is traveling becomes less, and participant time jumps forward."

"Right, got that part. So, how did you get from your audio waveform brainstorming idea to quantum communications?"

"We're basically adding those wavefunctions together and multiplying them by complex numbers to form new wave-functions, right? We were deriving those complex numbers by satisfying the normalization condition with our wavefunc-tions, where the wavefunction varied with momentum and time. And that's equivalent to varying space and time. So, there is our equation, see? Like this: We know the wavefield we are generating propagates to infinity and we know that every wavefield has a unique quantum signature. So, it's kinda like a quantum wave amplifier, where we are controlling the relative phase and magnitude."

"Ah, I see. The system can't fully replicate the entangle-ment state without the original analog source wave, but if you start with the original wave, you can reposition it using its quantum wave resonance signature, according to those wavefunctions."

"Yeah, that's the idea. It all kind of sprang from that. We pitched the idea to Rössler and he liked it enough to approve a go-ahead on the work. We determined that if we used three stations, we should be able to use them to triangulate a destination path anywhere within their planar space. And if NASA built one onto a satellite or a space station or whatever, we'd be able to triangulate anywhere within that massive set of 3D coordinates. So Rössler pitched it to them, and they liked it too. And—boom—they did it. And then George got caught making an unauthorized backup of the source code and was shown the door. Another guy, too."

"I can't believe they laid you off."

"Yeah. Actually, I got canned for helping George make an unauthorized jump. They were after him for making a backup of his own goddamned code."

"Whoops. What happened?"

"Well, big lawsuit. And then those bastards bombed the place. I think they suspected I was somehow involved. But then I won the lawsuit and agreed to settle if they gave me a job here, so here I am. Well, until June. They want us all to be out before hurricane season starts."

Li Yan nodded and added, "George really got the shitty end of the stick. After they made DNA tests a legal requirement, and the insurance companies started requiring them, George filed a grievance showing that, although he was below the requisite percentage of native American DNA—Navaho, I think it was—another major bloodline was Paleoindian from the Bering land bridge, which had previously had some sort of ruling that made it qualify. Anyway, he applied for First Nations rights, for housing, legal exemptions and all that. And then, the Supreme Court, like some goddamned Ministry of Racial Purity, ruled that he *wasn't* eligible, and all these other indigenous groups started challenging the ruling. Then, the feds in Canada really threw a wrench into it when they made discrimination based on genetics illegal, and this led them to cancel their First Nations-specific laws entirely. No special treatment for First Nations bloodlines at all. There was a huge uproar over that. This was followed by demands to do the same in the U.S. That went all the way up to the Supreme Court, but eventually it was outlawed here, too."

"Jeez. Well, good for Canada, I guess," said Amir.

"Ah, not really. The new laws took away an awful lot of aboriginal rights that really haven't seen a lot of compensatory relief. And it's the same here. George was only one of many who ended up a lot worse off than they had been."

Susan rolled her pen back and forth. When Li Yan had finished with her story, Susan changed the topic, hoping that she had not sounded tactless in doing so. "So, you were essentially using quantum resonance values to modify wave-function values?"

Li Yan nodded. "Yeah, but it only works if the quantum resonance value is the one that created the Alcubierre field's warp signature. We're not teleporting anyone just yet. But, hey, if you *move the field....*"

She snapped her fingers. "That quantum signature lets us

target an alternate set of coordinates. Long story short, we're able to solve for specific sets of space and time coordinates."

Karl was shaking his head. "But that's exactly why the NASA idea was genius. When you're talking about geographical coordinates, it's pretty dangerous to just jump there blind, of course. There is no opportunity to predict the integrity of the destination end. You might end up jumping straight into a pile of rubble or a nuclear wasteland."

Li Yan defended the idea. "True, but we can calculate geographic coordinates with acceptable accuracy. And we've developed transit pods that significantly reduce the risk. I admit it's probably best to avoid heavily populated or highly unstable areas, but logistically, pretty much everybody but Karl agrees that the risk level is acceptable for well-selected destination points."

She shrugged. "Trenton is not especially stable—there have been 14 quakes in the area since 1931—but its geological past is quite well known and the risk level of major quakes in the future is quite low—about two and a half percent over the next 50 years. We figured we could make a good estimate of its likely future over the next few thousand years. It seemed like a pretty safe bet."

"And then," said Karl, "the NASA guys blew us right out of the water by coming up with a way to set an entangled status bit. That made things a whole lot safer."

"But even that is never going to be completely safe," argued Li Yan.

"There've been accidents," admitted Karl, his mind flashing through the horrific imagery of those early site-cam videos. Impact Experiments one through seven. The Transit Pod collision tests. And that guy with the creepy hand.

"The one aspect of this I do like," he conceded, "is to take this idea a step further, and implement safety protocols and protective equipment that we specifically control. Way back in the early days, we started mandating an on-the-hour schedule for jumps, to minimize chances of collisions, and also to reduce site management costs. As we couldn't predict the condition of facilities in the future, the surest way to do that is to send the safety equipment forward with the travelers. In such a case, the ability to observe target site conditions during traversal and, if necessary, redefine temporal parameters 'on the fly' for a quantum wavefield becomes more practical; I have been an advocate of this as an idea worth exploring since way back when, well, since the first accident happened. I mean, imagine if you arrived to a poisonous atmosphere. You'd want that transit pod to keep you safe and rejump you right out of there ASAP."

"In fact, I had an idea a bit like that," said Susan. "I thought, 'wouldn't it be great if the platform and the pod sent messages back to the sending source. The platform, when cleared, would sent an 'OK to receive' status message after the outgoing stage is cleared. And the transit pod itself could send an 'OK' message when it is clear of the stage."

"So, if you *could* do that," said Karl, "you could have vehicles that carried a dynamically moving Alcubierre field as a destination point, allowing a sort of mobile time dilation. That would give you the ability to jump without a base station like this place."

He drew a curve on the white board, with a triangle on the line. "It's not that different from the original experiments, when we were doing those field displacement tests. The temporal data in the field still gets set at the origin point; the morphology of the wave itself is still subject to external forces, such as gravity, field effects, and so on. But you get the big advantage of safety, which is super important for very long jumps."

"Which would be awesome," agreed Susan. Amir nodded. emphatically

"Actually, I'm messing with you," confessed Karl. "We *are* doing that. We developed that with the funding from NASA. And it works. Your code is still in there. And don't tell anyone where you heard this, but rumor has it that there is a complete copy of the backup from George floating around out there. George supposedly uploaded it to a private server just before he was let go."

"What? So, there's a working backup out there in the wild?"

"It would seem so. Of course, it doesn't do all that much good without all the hardware specs and system design details. But, whaddaya know—that stuff subsequently ended up in the hands of a few interested parties in China, Russia and elsewhere. Normally, this would concern me, but honestly... those bastards at Andna deserved that."

"Unfortunately, the source code for the custom arrival point also fell into the hands of pirates, who began hijacking time-shifted shipments by redefining the destination time. There were some reports of whole shipments getting ghosted."

○ ○ ○

At that very moment, 25 years in the future, Dr. Eldon Johnson and a team of interdisciplinary scientists—including bio-physicists, chemists, molecular biologists, and genetic engineers—were encoding DNA sequence patches and other genetic packages for transfer back to his company's corporate headquarters. His company had made a vast fortune by patenting future innovations in this way.

○ ○ ○

"You know, I made backups to no less than five cloud-based products before I jumped. For safe keeping, you know, yeah? All five disappeared. It's only been—what, 25-something-years? I can't believe anybody trusted those goddamned things."

Susan sighed. "I still can't believe Rössler's gone."

"Ehh, it was natural causes. He should have jumped forward when he got cancer. It's no big deal now."

"I kind of regret that last meeting I had with him, where we had a bit of a blowout."

"I remember that! He threatened to sue you, didn't he?" asked Li Yan.

"Well, I *was* violating my NDA, I guess."

"At a closed-door meeting with the team leader on

company property? No." Li Yan rolled her chair back from the table. "He was just being a prick."

"I guess."

Karl was still focused on the main topic. "Ahem. As I was saying... so we started wondering whether you could do a motion vector calculation on, say, a spacecraft, and map the target timeline to a known destination point. In other words, if the source field emitter moves, could we jump to its future destination point?"

"Ohh, that would *so* useful. Do you think the field integrity control system would work in space, too?"

"Oh ya, it does. In fact, they proved that during those early ion thruster tests."

"Hmm," mused Susan. She tapped her pencil on a page of scribbled calculations.

"You're still restless," observed Li Yan.

"Yep. I'm going to do that big jump...soon. But maybe not right away. I'm going to sleep on it. If you guys are going back to Trenton, I'll probably do the jump there."

Li Yan eyed Amir. "And what about this handsome guy?"

"If it's safer now, I guess I'll go with Susan."

"We're kind of a team now," she laughed. She leaned closer to Li Yan's chair. "Why don't you and Karl come with us?"

"Oh, I really can't. I've promised a couple of key deliverables over the next two months. But maybe we could catch up with you later. How far do you think you'll go?"

Karl winked at Susan, then looked at Li Yan. "I've got a standing bet that she's going to take a really big leap one of these days. As I recall, I put my money on 383.67 years."

"I dunno yet," said Susan. "But yeah, there's a good chance."

○ ○ ○

It so happened that, at that precise moment, on the other side of the world, one of the recently opened commercial jump-stations in China was processing a new batch of incoming travelers.

A massive crowd, comprised primarily of refugees and immigrants who couldn't seem to get a fair shake in their own time, had jumped forward hoping to find a better new world in the future.

These were mostly economy travelers, taking advantage of lower costs for nighttime jumps.

When they arrived, massive camera arrays scanned the crowds and facial recognition databases pinpointed suspected terrorists, known criminals, sex offenders and other undesirables. Those who made it through the security checkpoints were herded through into a tradeshow area where third-rate educational institutions and predatory employers capitalized on their desperation.

○ ○ ○

Did you know?
92 percent of incoming travelers—or time-jumpers, as we call them—choose to end their journey here. These new citizens now contribute to our economy, providing benefits to all.

○ ○ ○

Did you know?
Fees are increasing for outgoing jumps. Beginning January 1, the transit fee will be $180,000 per adult. Ask about DNA discounts!

13

Deliberations and Decisions

Roughly 48 hours later, after much deliberation, Susan and Amir had decided to make the big jump together, using the new safety system. Karl and Li Yan declined to accompany them, but promised to "never say never."

Susan's deliberations had taken her thoughts back to Humanities class, to the words of Mahatma Gandhi: "Create and preserve the image of your choice." This seemed to Susan like a possible answer. Maybe the solution to a warring and greedy humanity was to achieve a more evolved state in one's personal life. Amir had been practicing meditation recently and had convinced Susan to try it too. She finally felt ready for the big jump.

Karl sounded like he wanted to do a few more small jumps forward first. "There's so much new information to assimilate," he confided. "It's about all I can manage. I just want to keep abreast of the latest research. And this *is* a great way to do that."

Two weeks later, he had negotiated a guaranteed position at the company's Trenton office in 8.17 years' time. The others bade him a fond farewell, not sure if they'd ever see him again.

o o o

8.17 years later, Karl showed up for work right on schedule. As was the standard procedure, he sat through the briefing session and learned—among other things—how common the use of fast-forward technologies by the transportation industry had become. The ones who made the most money in the short term were, ironically, those who exposed themselves to the greatest levels of rapid obsolescence. Entire industries built on highly perishable goods and ever-shorter delivery times were transformed by these technologies. Within a few years, the unemployment ranks swelled with now-underskilled members of the flash-forwarded workforce.

These were the workers least adept at managing the latest generation of AI-assistive technologies. By the time self-driving transport vehicles, delivery bots and automated restocking services had begun to dominate the transportation business, the underskilled couldn't even get a low-paying job in their former industry of choice.

Although touted in revisionist histories as an intentional move, the failure of the first 'massive language model' AIs to succeed in the area of executive-level business management was a bump on the path of progress. It's now looked at as more of a detour. "Humanized Psychology" AI became known as Business AI, designed to work within the scope of specifically targeted behaviors that were not always rational, such as desire, fear, greed and herd behavior. Mass AI became personal—and, we like to think, more ethical—when we began intelligence augmentation as an individualized bio-engineering service. As the business world filled with ego-bots, behaviorists specifically deprioritized the ego-like attributes of Personal AI for the overall benefit of society. It became the AI for the rest of us.

"There's a lot to show you and tell you about and I don't to overwhelm you."

A serving bot rolled into the room, dressed like a waiter.

"You dress them up now?"

The new intern seemed taken aback. "Uh, sure. For special occasions. Like this!" The bot rolled closer and extended its tray.

"Are you hungry or thirsty? May I offer you some cheese... and wine, perhaps?"

"Sure, thanks," said Karl, unaware that the bot was mapping his body in 3D as it rolled to and fro around him.

"My name is Andrea," offered the intern. "And this—" she gestured toward the screen on the wall— "is the briefing center. It's part of our trade agreement with our friends upstairs."

"More cheese, sir?" asked the robot.

"Mmm, yes."

Karl looked at Andrea's beautiful young face and body. He was probably close to twice her age, but she was definitely his type. "That is *very* good cheese," he said to her. "Have you tried it?"

"We're not supposed to eat on the job, sir," she said with a polite smile.

"I won't tell if you want to give it a try."

"No thank you, sir."

Actually, a washroom would be really great, too," said Karl.

"Ah, of course. Right over there."

While Karl was out of the room, Andrea switched the input source at her console and inspected the security cam segments on the display screen more closely. There weren't cameras in the washroom, but a locator showed him moving around and, as soon as he exited the room, he again appeared onscreen. By the time Karl returned, Andrea was nonchalantly looking out the window. She picked up a tablet and approached him as he entered the room.

"You have been flagged in a video. Would you like to see it?" said Andrea, handing the tablet to Karl.

"What is it?" asked Karl.

"It's a video feed from a couple of our security cams. You know this man, I think?"

In the video, a well-dressed man on a video conferencing screen spoke to a seated man—it was George! —in the cold blue-white light of a vast room filled with rack-mounted computers.

"This room was clearly marked as a restricted area for authorized personnel only. Why did you attempt to enter this area?"

"I was just looking for a washroom."

"Are you aware that trespassing in a restricted area is a serious offence?"

George ignored the question. "Ugh, you people work in this light?" he moaned. "Can't you take the brightness down?"

The well-dressed man on the screen spoke again. "We have optimized the lighting in our server center for maximum power efficiency," he explained rather earnestly. "It looks like a freaking grow-op from here," grumbled George.

Yeah, that's our George, thought Karl. But he gave no indication that he knew him.

When the clip ended, Karl handed the tablet back to Andrea. "Is this, uh, person still here?"

"No, I'm afraid he's moved on," said Andrea.

"Well, when was this?"

Just then, the same well-dressed man that had appeared in the video appeared on the larger display monitor hanging on the wall and addressed Karl.

"Mister Schraeder, we have more information on file about you than we do about Mister Gomez, who we believe was once a member of your working group. It would seem that some of his records are missing. And we are...investigating...a possible security breach."

Karl scrutinized the monitor, suddenly suspicious. Gomez, eh? Why was George going by an alias?

"We are told he has a keen interest in AI systems and technologies."

"Well, uh... What kind of security breach?"

"Unfortunately, we are not at liberty to share that information with you at this time. Your cooperation is appreciated, and your security clearance will be processed accordingly."

"I do have a job here, don't I?"

"All the necessary permissions should be in place within the hour; our apologies for any inconvenience. Please take a seat here in the lobby. Would you like a hot or cold beverage?"

"No thank you."

"Your mandatory briefing session takes approximately 30 minutes. Would you like to attend the session beginning in five minutes?"

"Yes, I would, thank you," said Karl. He felt optimistic for the first time in ages.

A few minutes before the briefing session, Andrea led him into a room with three large curved video screens, where the presentation began precisely on time. During the briefing, Karl could scarcely believe what he was hearing. The advances in AI and automated surveillance systems were impressive, but the advances in bio-augmentation in just eight years were staggering.

"Research facilities around the world have been working on artificial intelligence for several decades, with most of the big advances in deep learning and massive language models coming in the first few decades of the 21st century. Recently, we have pivoted from our early efforts in that area into the area of augmented intelligence. And now, after more than a decade of work, we have a product that truly takes us to the forefront of this exciting new frontier."

"The results have been overwhelmingly positive, although augmentation does introduce some societal friction, you might say. Put simply, we make people smarter—a *lot* smarter. It's been great for research, math, science, and a great many areas in which engineering and programming are relevant. Even the arts have generally benefitted, but there are areas that could be better, so of course, we look at this as a work in progress. We've tried to avoid indoctrinating people into beliefs in imaginary gods and monsters. Instead, we create our own here."

"You'll be working on a program we call the Elephant's Memory. It's where people who want to get deep into augmented reality will one day live and work. Basically, they will plug in and run programs that serve as the front end to their personal reality."

o o o

14

The Big One

Not-quite-exactly 383.67 years later, Susan and Amir sat in the same room for a different briefing. Even the chairs looked the same.

"Before we begin," said the session leader, "Please note: the elevators and stairwells leading upstairs from this area of the building are currently blocked and inaccessible. Do *not* attempt to leave this building via the stairs or elevators. After the session, please exit via the Annex hallway marked A1 *only*."

At the briefing, they learned about the emerging proto-racial group known as the Evolvists (or more colloquially, "Volvists"). This group was primarily comprised of those between the ages of 19 and 35, who deliberately infected themselves with retrovirus-based change-agents designed to temporarily or permanently alter one's DNA. Volvist modders were the party crowd, with their phosphorescent party hair and tweaked pheromones on weekends, but the serious cultists were into ornamental body mods and cross-species hybridism.

Early efforts to demonize the so-called "Infex" and ban these and similar DNA-based mods led to a strong backlash and by the end of the century, the majority of children born were at least partly hybridized with what became known as Managed DNA.

There was also a presentation on popular career choices. One of the latest hot jobs was as a Digital End User Experience (DEUX) Designer. These people worked with AR shader and filter devs to craft augmented realities that appealed to the masses. The shader devs added visual and audio details, such as environmental lighting enhancements or ambient audio replacements; the filter devs removed unwanted details. Background replacements were the #1 DEUX category most months, with political and sports-oriented front ends topping the charts in the run-up periods before elections and major sporting events.

"The most profound manifestation of our ongoing research effort has been the great work done by our volunteers —people like you—on what we call the Restoration Project," said the presenter.

"As many of you know, about 400 years ago, there was a massive, catastrophic internet-based attack that corrupted a lot of information systems. Almost everything that was exploitable—which, as it turned out, was almost everything— was taken out more or less simultaneously. Every database, every platform, every server, they all went down at once, in what we now call the Omega Event."

Amir leaned close to Susan's right ear and whispered. "That can't even happen. Can it?"

She shrugged.

The presenter continued. "It was pure pandemonium. Virtually every system that was connected to or accessible via the internet during that time became a victim of this attack."

"Sounds like it did," Susan whispered back.

"When it hit, the attack spread from the top-level domain on down. You see, the internet was like a monoculture in those days. Nearly everything, everywhere ran on one of a few dozen different architectures. And this thing had working exploits for all of them. The big one, of course, was the top-level domain name system. That was the first to go. Once the system's top-level servers were compromised, much of the activity that followed was hidden.

"One minute, everything looked normal—on the spoofed servers. Eight seconds later: boom, they switched back to the real servers, and everything there had already been permanently scrambled. It happened so fast, the deed was done before emergency mitigation efforts had even begun. Few thought an attack like this was even possible. But it did a *lot* of damage.

"It exploited a design feature of the top-level servers themselves: Permission levels can only be created in the top-level site of a site collection and by default they are available in every site in the site collection. Thus, when the hackers created the new permission level it became available in all sub-sites.

"And in this case, *all* the connections to the Top-Level Domains had been spoofed. And all the transport layer protocols and data streams looked normal to them, and everything matched the source, so no one noticed the fakes. And this top-level attack essentially took down the entire internet, everywhere. It hit everyone simultaneously, worldwide.

"At the time, it was called the first AI-led cyber-attack, although that label has been greatly misused in recent decades. These days, it's remembered by those in the financial markets as the Great Fall.

"Theories abounded as to how such a massive spoof could have been pulled off. There were rumors that the global banking systems had been compromised; cryptocurrency blockchains were exploited across all exchanges. It re-infected systems as soon as restored backups were put online. And the more they looked, the more evidence of its incredible sophistication they found.

"It wasn't limited to a particular platform, or a particular unpatched vulnerability. A huge library of exploits no one even knew existed were all mass-deployed at once while the Top-Level Domains were simultaneously rerouted to rogue servers. Exactly what happened next is a matter of speculation, but we think the TLDs were switched over to copies that made everything look like it was all right, while a massive and highly automated brute-force hacking effort was going on behind the façade. At the time, it seemed incomprehensible that any system could replicate the entire internet, but when the fake TLDs finally flipped back to the real ones, almost everything was encrypted—and unlike other ransomware, an option to pay a ransom to unlock and restore the encrypted data was never offered.

"There was speculation that hackers somehow commandeered the big homeland security systems in the U.S. (Mae East and Mae West being the most well-known examples) that almost everything on the internet went through in those days. But however they did it—and we still don't know who 'they' were—the attack destroyed unprecedented amounts of data; it was a real wake-up call to a society almost totally dependent on the internet for everything from commerce and taxation to healthcare and schooling. The stock market crashed; economies and even entire nations went dark. The news media—what was left of it anyway—called it the datapocalypse. The Omega Event.

"Our request to all of you is to share your knowledge of your history, your culture, and your expertise with us, in order that we may rebuild and restore our lost and damaged historical archives.

"We have set up public archives to make it easy to contribute to The Restoration Project and we offer compensation for valuable historical information or resources. Please share the past for a better future."

The slogan dominated every screen in the hall.

"Our New Historians are looking forward to speaking with you. You will receive a training credit just for signing up. Please schedule your session today. The world depends on you!

"And that's the end of our presentation today. Thank you all for attending!"

"We should probably register to help them fill in their history of our time."

"I guess so," said Amir. "Hey, I've been wondering about that thing Karl was talking about—the NASA invention that allowed them to send status bits back to the departure point. We could use that to let people know we're ok, right? So why didn't we ever receive any of those messages back then?"

Susan thought for a moment. "Perhaps it doesn't work like that, unless you have already built the capability to listen for such signals, in which case the NASA site would be as far back as that invention can reach."

"Hmm, I suppose. Or maybe it just doesn't work."

A middle-aged woman in a blue dress took the microphone and spoke to the crowd. "Please help yourselves to our wonderful selection of traditional cheese snacks."

"Hey, Li Yan!" Amir shouted and waved excitedly to a face in the crowd. She heard him and headed over and gave him a hug and a big smile. She hadn't changed much—still rocking that blue streak and showing off the tattoos. No wedding ring, though. Susan hugged her warmly. She looked happy.

"Wow, wonderful to see you here. When did you jump?"

Susan showed off her jump visa. "Just today."

She looked at Amir. "Are you here with anyone else?"

"No."

"Have you heard anything from Karl—or any of the others?"

"I don't know about the others, but Karl's here, somewhere. He and I both jumped here earlier this week. He's tracking George. That's why we're here."

"Really?! Fantastic."

"Yeah, just a minute and I'll find him." She pulled a device from her pocket and unfolded the screen. Amir was delighted to find *someone* with a working phone. "Ah, hey Karl," she said. "There's someone here to see you."

"Okay, great. I'll be there in two minutes."

"He'll be here in a moment, he says."

Li Yan leaned close to Susan's ear. "So, I have to ask: are you guys an item?"

"Oh gosh, no," said Susan.

"Why not? He's so cute," laughed Li Yan. Susan watched with amusement as Li Yan cornered Amir and made small talk with him. He didn't stand a chance.

When Karl arrived, he entered the room via the door on the far side of the room. At that distance, Susan thought it must be the lighting. His skin looked decidedly blue. But as he walked closer, the bluish hue was unmistakable.

"Wow, long time no see. I guess it doesn't seem that long."

"It's fantastic to see you. I wasn't sure if we'd ever see you again."

"We?! Wait—what did I miss? Did you marry Amir or something?"

This caught Susan off-guard. "No no, we're just... In fact, he's... well, I don't know exactly where he is. But I came here with him, so he's around somewhere."

"You're looking well."

"You too, but..."

"You're wondering about the blue, right? Ya, well, it's kind of a funny story. There was this malware, you see, it was basically a malicious retrovirus, engineered to produce certain, ah, changes. A few years ago, the antidote—I guess you could call it—to this virus was this ridiculous commercial scam, where you had to keep paying, or the dormant virus would re-activate and reinfect you, turning you blue again. It was kind of a social stigma thing, nobody wanted to be blue, so they paid. But, hey, I said screw it, I had this girlfriend at the time, she was happy being blue and I was too. And then the goddamn company went out of business and the antidote site shut down. There are some, ah, generic providers, but they all seem to have freaky side effects. And it's all done with encrypted blockchain bullshit that makes it all-but-impossible to view the code. And they're insanely expensive, of course. So, I'm in the fucking blue class and that's why."

"Anyway, it's great to see you. You know, you might be able to help me with a little math problem I'm having. It's kind of related to blockchain stuff, in fact. You familiar with that?"

Susan shrugged. "A little bit. I never got too far into cryptocurrencies, beyond studying the technical aspects in school. Is it still a thing?"

"Heh. You probably didn't hear the big news. Some of that first- and second-gen stuff had a hidden feature—a massively-parallel hardware decryption feature, using consumer electronics running cryptocurrency software as the "hosts" of the concealed cipher-breaking effort. It eventually came out that an unknown entity—presumably the government, although of course they denied it was them—was using the blockchain processing stream to decode other encrypted data streams, presumably those belonging to foreign governments or, you know, persons of interest. It was found to be surreptitiously inserting commands into the blockchain, to temporarily insert other commands into the processing queue. They were using the aggregate cloud's processing power for purposes completely unrelated to the blockchain. It's an interesting idea—how do you manage to get a worm to run for extended periods of time, without people taking it offline? Run it inside a popular monetary system! It actually had its conceptual roots in a 1991 thought experiment known as the Chinese Lottery."

"That's very interesting. I suppose they'll go over that at the next monthly briefing session?"

"Oh, unfortunately, this is the last one. That's why there's wine and cheese and whatnot. It's a wrap party. They've canceled the whole program. Too many underskilled workers were coming in, it was becoming a political hot potato—a real budgetary nightmare."

He refilled his glass and poured one for her, too. "Cheers. Oh ya, there was kind of a scandalous story about us on the news, how people were committing crimes then we were helping them time travel away; oops, we're not allowed to even *say* 'time travel' anymore—to hell with that."

He's drunk.

"The company brought it on themselves. People were doing these ridiculous long plays, taking advantage of compound interest and whatnot. It's really shitty how they're treating you guys these days. They cracked down on life insurance, medical coverage, unemployment, retirement, all that stuff. It's a total rip-off. And the really sick people keep jumping forward, in hope of an eventual cure."

Karl sighed and looked at Susan, still young and beautiful in her nerdy-girl way. She always looks like she wants to leave.

Susan had just noticed that Amir's coat was gone from the back of his chair. And so was Li Yan's.

"Hey," said Karl, tapping on her shoulder. "You won't believe what I found. You will go nuts when you see this, I promise you. It's just crazy. Do you want to see it?"

The wine might have been partially to blame, but she said yes. Curiosity had gotten the best of her. Maybe something could still surprise her after all.

o o o

"This way," said Karl, leading her down the long hall from the big room in L1.

"Where are we going?"

He handed her a small flashlight and produced another one from a pocket on the leg of his cargo pants. "You'll see. Lots of interesting things here." As they reached the control area, Karl pointed the beam of light at a series of pipes and, beside them, large banks of solar batteries. "For starters, look at this: the whole place has been converted to run on geothermal energy and—apparently—solar power. That's new."

"Looks mostly intact. Do you think it still runs?"

"The system is offline but it we could try rebooting once we get the power on. And hey, this is great: the vacuum chamber integrity is still at 100 percent. After all this time. Amazing."

"Do you think there's a decent chance we might be able to get this baby up and running?"

"I dunno. For better or worse, the accelerator itself doesn't look that much different than when I last worked on it—it looks like they just discontinued the program and let it gather dust. But hey, I doubt there's anyone else around here who understands all this ancient tech as well as we do."

Just then, Karl's phone buzzed. "Oh hey. Yes. She's here. Ya, we're not far from you, just come up to the old control room in L1. No, I know. It's okay. I brought flashlights."

"Ah, this looks familiar." The L1 information desk area was at least recognizable, although the D had fallen off the ancient ANDNA sign.

A moment later, a pair of figures stepped out of the darkness. It was Amir and Li Yan.

"Karl!"

"Hey, Amir!"

"What are you doing here?" asked Li Yan.

"I'm just showing Susan what we found the other day."

"Have you shown her what's upstairs yet?"

"No, not yet," said Karl.

Susan shook her head, her imagination now running into the darker possibilities.

"We have been following George's markers for a while now," explained Karl. He's made some big jumps. And you guys, too. Remind me to show you how to read the jump codes."

"Sounds good. I've been documenting the changes made to the system, and tracking the business."

Amir put it right out there. "They sued you?"

"Yeah. They found out I was going to expose the scummier side of their business: the accidents, the coercion programs and that whole Andna thing. Did you know that they got tax credits from the government for reducing the numbers of people on social services? The government actively sought to defer its own problems by simply shoving the least productive parts of society out of the equation. Andna made money on everyone they sent after year three, when their mandate changed from research to revenue."

"You were documenting the system as it evolved?"

"Well, I obtained all the patent docs, and they posted a lot of technical notes over the years. I have a fairly recent copy of a full operations manual. You know, not much changed substantially after the first four decades or so."

"You've got to be kidding. The system's almost four hundred years old."

"There were lots of minor changes, of course. They swapped all the closed-source OS bits out for open-source around year five. Then they reversed that decision again—idiots—a few years later. They upgraded a lot of the electronics, of course—the server farms, the AI stuff. I had no insight into the details of that stuff, but I'm sure the changes there were massive."

"But the only really big changes that happened in the next hundred years was the conversion to geothermal and solar energy."

"Yeah, we saw that."

"One of the patents they held was for a super-long-life

battery design—it was still experimental at the time I was there, but apparently, these batteries were designed to last several thousand years. They encased small amounts of radioactive material in manufactured diamonds and built them into batteries that could supply power for the entire period of radioactive decay. We're talking about still having a 50% battery charge after several thousand years. Not cheap to produce, but amazingly efficient—and shielded, so they probably won't kill us. And get this," he said excitedly, opening a drawer at one of the desks. "I found a whole drawer full of them right here. They used to stock the pods with them. Do you want a few? Might come in handy."

"Thanks," said Amir, taking two.

"I'll pass," said Susan, warily.

"So, the whole place became quite self-sufficient. And, from what I've seen, it worked exactly as intended. Nothing much has changed in 300-odd years. I'll be very surprised if there's anything significantly different now."

"Well, they made a temple out of it," noted Li Yan.

"That *is* different."

"Come on, I'll show you."

"So, I guess the control room must be behind that wall?"

Amir shrugged. "The layout's the same as the original facility?"

"It's pretty much identical. The only thing that really changed was the security around the front entrance. After that nutjob drove his van through the front window at the original facility, they redesigned that whole area."

"Yeah, it was a mess when we got there. That's why we came here."

"Ya, I figured." Karl's flashlight illuminated a table just to the right of the elevator. Hey, Amir," Karl said. "Can you help me move this? It will make it easier for us to climb up. Up against the elevator here. Okay—that's good."

They helped Susan climb up onto the heavy table. Light flashed off the shiny interior surfaces of the elevator as she poked her head inside the half-open doors and clambered up onto the raised elevator floor." See how close the ceiling is there?" said Karl, pointing the light toward the top of the elevator. "Can you reach the hatch?"

"Yeah, I think so."

"Be careful," cautioned Li Yan. "There are some sharp edges on that grille."

"All right," said Karl. Once you're up there, just climb the ladder until you get to the next floor and wait for us there.

Susan climbed up until she came to a narrow doorway covered by what seemed to be some sort of heavy cloth.

She pushed the cloth aside and squeezed through the half-open doors there, emerging from behind an ornate tapestry on the wall. At least it wasn't pitch-black up here. Light streamed into the room from the nearby windows. A moment later, Li Yan and Amir followed, with Karl bringing up the rear.

"So this used to be M1?" marveled Susan. The lobby was completely different than she remembered it. "Whoa, it's really different. Wasn't there a stairwell there?"

"I'll bet you it's right behind that wall."

"What the hell is this place?"

"Crazy, huh?" said Karl.

It was ornately decorated in richly colored tapestries and golden arches. "And they said we'd never see in the golden arches in this neighborhood," joked Karl.

"It's bizarre," marveled Amir. "It's like a church."

"I told you it was completely bonkers, didn't I?" said Karl.

"Well, you sure weren't kidding. Wow." She looked at the motifs on the tapestries on the walls and signs on what appeared to be an altar. "What's all this stuff about 'Anna?'"

"I think it's their god, or something like that."

"But how could whoever built this place not be aware that this elevator was here?"

"Li Yan and I pried the door open just a few days ago when we first climbed up here."

"Yeah," said Li Yan. "We just pried and pulled until at last we managed to open the door wide enough to squeeze through. It was really stuck, so it's not surprising that they never realized it was movable."

Amir and Susan wandered the floor, marveling at the lavish decorations. "It's like an altar."

"Oh, I think that's exactly what it is," said Li Yan.

"I don't think they ever realized these panels were an elevator. They just covered them up. And look there, where the emergency exit stairs were. They are completely blocked by that wall. So they probably never realized there was a room full of equipment down there."

"Shh! What was that?" whispered Li Yan. "I think someone's coming. Hide!" Karl and Li Yan quickly retreated into the elevator shaft behind the tapestry. But Susan and Amir, on the other side of the room had no good places to hide.

They vainly tried to hide behind the altar as two guards appeared. One pointed at them threateningly. "You there. Come with us. Both of you."

o o o

15

A Puzzle in the Antechamber

A guard entered the Council chamber. At the front of the room, five members of the high council sat behind a long table on a raised platform flanked by decorative tapestries. An aide stood at each end of the table. One of the aides whispered into the ear of the Chief Councillor, who was sitting in the table's center seat.

The Councillor gestured to the guard. "Step closer," he commanded.

"I am told," the Councillor said, "that you captured a pair of intruders in the antechamber of the old temple. How did they get in there?"

The guard looked uneasy as he stepped forward to speak. "I beg the pardons of the Council," he began, "I was responsible for guarding the entrance to the temple and at no time was the entrance left unattended. I saw no one enter."

The councilwoman nearest the other aide frowned and

looked at the Chief Councillor. She then addressed the guard. "How can you explain that?" she asked. "Could they have entered the building earlier, perhaps the night before?"

"The building was under constant surveillance, Councillor. We did, however, interrogate the intruders about what they were doing in there."

"Well? What did they say?"

The guard tugged at his glove nervously as he spoke. "They insist they did not intrude willfully and have repeatedly stated that they mean no harm."

"And you believe them?!" declared the Councillor, incredulously. "Did they say anything else?"

In truth, Councillor," said the guard, "They said they were *just looking* at the building."

The councilwoman looked exasperated.

"Bring them in," ordered the Chief Councillor.

The guard signaled to the guards at the door and they escorted Susan and Amir into the chamber to stand before the high council.

"Step forward," commanded the Chief Councillor as he gestured to them. "What are your names and what were you doing in the temple?"

"My name is Susan and this is my associate, Amir."

Amir smiled hopefully. "We want to assure you that we meant no harm or disrespect. We were just looking around."

"Ridiculous," muttered the councilman on the left.

"How did you get inside the temple?"

Amir looked nervously into Susan's eyes and almost

imperceptibly shook his head as she stammered to find a plausible sounding explanation. "We... were, uh..."

Amir wiped his brow and swallowed.

The Councillor eyed their clothing suspiciously. "And where are you from? Have you journeyed from somewhere far away?"

"Well, no, not exactly," said Amir.

Susan raised her finger, eager to speak.

"May I try to explain?" she asked.

"Please do."

Susan decided to try a more positive approach. "We arrived in the temple by a form of travel that is difficult to explain. We would like to share our knowledge with you, but we ask for your patience while we explain how it works."

"Can you demonstrate this for us here and now?"

"I wish we could," muttered Amir, very quietly.

The Chief Councillor thought for a moment and then asked: "Did you appear from within a magical whirlwind?"

"Well, yes, I guess you might say that," she admitted.

His eyes widened.

"It is the prophecy fulfilled," whispered the Councillor sitting to his left.

Oh boy, thought Amir. Now she's done it. "It is not magic," he began, "and we are not magicians."

"Silence!" demanded the Chief Councillor, examining Susan's book. She grimaced as he tore a page from the book and turned to the aide standing at the end of the table. "Find Kaedra. And take this to His Eminence."

o o o

The footsteps echoed loudly in the chamber halls as the courier hurried past rows of doors and beneath vaulted ceilings of the passageways between the Entremain and the Council Hall.

Above, on each side of the halls, the stained-glass windows glowed dully with the waning light of the auburn sky.

Two guards stood outside the door of the High Chamber. As the courier approached, they moved to block the door and stood there, their imposing figures towering threateningly over her tiny frame. The Chambermaster rushed over, his finger raised. "Uh-uh. *Never* go in without checking in first at *this* desk," he admonished her.

"I have an urgent message for His Eminence from the Chief Councillor," she said breathlessly.

He eyed the envelope. "*I'll* take that."

He put a hand heavy with ornate rings on her shoulder and turned her around. "Thank you for your service, child. You will surely be blessed. You may go now."

After the courier left, he held the envelope up toward the light for a few seconds, then signaled the guards to return to their positions with a waggle of his index finger and pressed the latch of the door handle.

"Your Eminence," the Chambermaster said as he bowed his head. "I bring you an urgent missive from the Chief Councillor."

From the podium, a wizened hand motioned for the Chambermaster to approach. He passed the package to the hand that waited, waved his bejeweled hand ceremoniously, bowed again, and left without another word.

As the door of the chamber clicked shut, expectant hands moved the ornate silver letter-opener beneath the flap on the envelope.

When the package was open, the papers within—an uncommonly ugly foolscap, thought the Lord of the High Chamber—were withdrawn and laid on the table before him. He placed the opener at the side of the desk and pulled the candelabra closer. He adjusted his spectacles and began to read.

His eyes narrowed as he scanned the paragraphs on the small page. His wizened right hand ran over the torn edges of the ring-binding holes. He read the lines again—and again. He flipped the paper over, then held the paper to the flame. As it burned to ash, he thumped his jewel-laden chalice on the podium.

The Chambermaster rushed back into the room. "How may I be of service, Your Eminence?"

"Call the Council to session," he commanded. "Advise the members of the Council that the prophecy is true."

"May there be many blessings upon you, Eminence, for thou art alive and with us always," said the Chambermaster as he bowed his head and backed out of the room.

"May Anna lead us to righteousness. Amen."

○ ○ ○

A special meeting of the Annatarian High Council was

called that very evening. As the members gathered in the Antechamber, there was both confusion and excitement.

"I have heard that His Eminence may attend," whispered one. "That *would* be unusual," said another. Many shared what they had heard whispered in the corridors: a prophecy had been fulfilled and a miracle had occurred.

As the bells rang, the Council convened before the Chief Councillor.

"The Council calls upon the Chambermaster."

The Chambermaster stood up from his seat at the long table and waved his hand ceremoniously toward the Chief Councillor. "I am honored to bring glad tidings to you all from His Eminence, with whom I spoke just this morning. And I have wonderful news: there has been a miracle in the Temple of The Ancients. The Ancients have spoken, as long prophesied, bringing tidings of joy and a message of peace."

"May The One be blessed, for he is alive and with us always."

Indeed, The One had been alive and with them a miraculously long time. It was a story handed down from generation to generation, how He had lived for more than 400 years— surely a miracle. And the storytellers taught how he had bravely ventured into the forbidden underworld and received the holy word of Anna and her talismans of eternal light. And now, another of his wondrous prophecies had come true!

"They say they are not familiar with our ways. And they claim to have arrived in a magical whirlwind, as The One prophesied long ago. And one even carries the Talisman of the Eternal Light."

Some on the Council couldn't believe what they were hearing. Within moments, the Council chamber erupted into arguments.

"And where are these Ancients who have spoken? Can we, too, see them and hear them? Or is this just another promise of the glorious times to come?"

"It must be a deception—a trick. We must forever be vigilant, for the evil ones cannot be trusted."

"You doubt The One?"

"Order, order!" cried the Chief Councillor.

"They say they come in peace—and they don't want to cause any trouble."

"That's what the evil ones always say," mumbled one of the Councillors.

"Perhaps torturing one of them...?" another suggested.

"Let Kaedra speak with them. She will find out if they speak the truth."

The Chief Councillor turned to the silver-haired woman to his left. "Kaedra, can you do this?" he asked. She bowed her head gracefully. "It shall be done. Give them some dinner and then bring them to my garden-house and I will speak with them there."

○ ○ ○

It was dark by the time the coach-driver delivered Susan and Amir to the home of Kaedra Wen. When they arrived, he led them around the side of the main house, past the garden, to a small but elegant garden-house. A moment later, a woman with dark skin and silvery hair opened the door. She was carrying a teapot. It was a warm evening and she was dressed in a gown covered in floral patterns. She set down the pot and unstacked cups for all three of them. "A warm greeting," she said, extending her hands toward both of them. "I am Kaedra Wen." Susan and Amir tentatively reciprocated, each holding a hand for a few seconds while introducing themselves.

"Please make yourselves comfortable," said Kaedra. "I trust they fed you well?"

Amir smiled amiably. "Yes, thank you."

She turned to Susan. "And was your journey here pleasant enough?" Susan smiled and nodded, her mind racing through this hairpin turn of events since their capture. Kaedra held the teapot up. "Would you like a cup of tea?"

"Oh yes."

Kaedra handed her a cup.

"Thank you," said Susan. "You call it tea, do you?"

"Yes, what do you call it?"

"Oh, we call it tea, too," laughed Susan. "It is true, though, that some of our words have meanings that might be hard to understand. Do you know what 'science' is?"

"Is it a story of the way things are?"

"Well, I guess that's one way of looking at it. The way we think of it, science is the understanding of why the things we observe are the way they are. The 'magic' is the data and the science is in the understanding of it, of *how it works*. This provides us with a framework to make predictions about how things we do not yet know about will behave. From this, we built a better understanding of our world. We call these people *scientists*. In fact, *we*—she gestured to Amir—work with many scientists. Perhaps you have people who already do this?"

"No, we do not have… scientists. But we do have story-tellers—and you are good storyteller."

"That's very kind of you to say that. Anyway, from that understanding, our scientists gained the insight they needed to build a time machine to open a kind of a shortcut to the future—like a gateway to tomorrow. And they sent us through it. Here."

"Time machine, hmm. I have not heard of such a thing. Is it related to 'magic'?"

"No, although our time machine might seem like magic, I suppose."

"There are many different kinds of machines," offered Amir, trying to help. "They help us do various things. Uh, for example, perhaps a machine made this teacup?"

"Oh no," said Kaedra, who knew full well what machines were. "An orb tree made that cup."

"Ah, well," he smiled, feeling that they were making progress. "There are machines that make teacups where we came from."

"You have no trees?"

"We do, but perhaps not exactly like this… orb tree." Susan admired the cup (unaware that it was made from genet-ically engineered hairless coconut, which had become more common in the northeast of the republic in recent years). "Very nice."

She decided to try a more direct approach. "Do you know

of any place where people or things appear or disappear as if by magic?"

"There are stories."

"Can we see these stories?"

"They are not written down. But we have a storyteller. She will hear your stories and if she believes you, she will tell you ours. It will soon be time for the children's stories. I will ask her if she can hear your story immediately afterwards." Susan seemed hesitant. "Come! A good story *needs* good listeners. She should be starting very soon...."

o o o

"Once upon a time," said the Storyteller, "there was a little girl named Slumberina, who lived in a great big pit. She didn't really mind living in a pit, because she had the nicest bed you've ever seen. It was as big as most people's houses, and as soft and bouncy as a marshmallow. It was so big, her mother and father had to build a special room in the pit just to hold it! And Slumberina liked nothing better in the world than her big beautiful bed."

She paused and opened her eyes very wide.

"And what do *you* think she like to do in that big, beautiful bed?" she asked the children.

"She liked to jump on it!" said one, much to the delight of the others.

"Make a tent under the covers!" said another.

"That sounds like fun. Anything else?"

"Make babies?" The others roared with laughter.

"Really? Oh my goodness!"

"Well, *I* heard that this great big bed was filled with the down of 10,000 geese, and it had 100 pillows, as light and fluffy as the clouds on a summer day. Slumberina loved to stay in bed all day and night long and do nothing at all but sleep, sleep, sleep.

"And do you know why? It certainly wasn't because she was tired. Slumberina slept more than anybody. Nobody else could sleep half as long as Slumberina. They had work to do, or games to play, or places to go — but Slumberina just stayed in bed.

"The reason she slept so much was that Slumberina loved to dream. In fact, she would rather dream about places than actually go to them, for she had decided that, if you actually went somewhere, there were all sorts of things that could go wrong. If you went to the park, it might be raining, or, if you went to see a play, it might be sold out. In her dreams, the plays were never sold out, and the weather was always just right.

"Dreaming was especially good for some things. Take flying, for instance. Slumberina loved to fly, but she didn't need a giant feather to ride on or even wings in her dreams, and she never fell or hurt herself. She could jump as high as she liked, and just float there, in the air, like a big balloon.

"Because she never went out in the sun, Slumberina's skin became paler and paler, until it was as white as snow. And because she never played with other children, she didn't have any friends at all. Slumberina never went out to play, or jump rope or run, or climb a tree, so she never even thought to dream about any of these things. She just had her pillows to hug, and her dreams to keep her company.

"One day, in between two or three dreams, Slumberina's ears started to hear a sound they hadn't heard before. It was the sound of children playing; only Slumberina didn't know that, as she'd never played with real children.

"So she invited all her new friends over and they all climbed on top of her big bouncy bed and jumped as high as they liked. And when they were at the very top of each jump, for just a moment, they could just float there, like a hundred happy balloons.

"And do you know what? They jumped so high, they jumped right out of that pit, up into the bright blue sky, and they landed in the soft green grass. 'It's so beautiful!' she exclaimed. And everyone smiled. And they never went back to that dark old pit.

The End.

Time for bed, children. Good night."

o o o

16

Causal Chains and Fractal Planes

After the children had all left, Kaedra spoke to the Storyteller in private for a moment and then departed. The Storyteller held out her hand. "My name is Ceryl Wen and I am honored to hear your story."

Susan pressed her hand against Ceryl's but did not grip it. "Hello Ceryl. My name is Susan, and this is Amir."

"You have pale skin, Susan. Why is it not like ours, or that of your companion? Are you from... the pits?" The question hung there awkwardly for a few seconds until she winked and they realized it was a joking reference to her story for the children.

Amir was visibly amused as he clasped her hand in both of his. "There aren't any pale-skinned people in this area? Wow, a lot has changed."

Susan tried to explain. "What he means is, there used to be. Where we come from, storytellers write their stories down onto paper, into books of knowledge. They tell stories of events that happened, and many other kinds of stories. Stories of the actions of people and the places they came from—and where they went. Are there any books here?”

“We have no books. Do you have one we can see?”

“Well, I have this one here that I’m using to keep notes about the places and people we’ve seen on our journey.”

“That is good. Tell me a story from your book, then.”

“Well,” Susan began, “not all books necessarily contain stories. Sometimes, books express ideas or convey information. For example....” She opened her notebook to a blank page. On it, she drew a point.

“This dot here,” she began, “is our starting point. Let’s pretend that we have an unlimited supply of dots just like this one. And we put them all in the same place. All right here. There’s none to the left or the right, in the front or back, or above or below. There’s no direction to any of the other dots. They all fit exactly in that one dot’s non-directional space. Now, if our dots went in two different places, then we could start to see that they went in a particular direction. Some over here, some over there. If we have two of those no-dimensional points, and we start to fill in all the points between them, then we end up with a line of points that becomes what we think of as a one-dimensional line. And if we put more dots along that line, it fills in that one-dimensional line. But...if we have three points and they are *not* all in a straight line, we will get the start of a *two*-dimensional shape, known as a plane. Like this piece of paper, with dots here, here and here. Okay?”

“Yes, okay.”

Ceryl nodded.

Susan tore the page out of the book. "Now, this page represents our two-dimensional surface, and we crumple it up. As it becomes more and more crumply, it starts to become *three* dimensional—it has height, width *and* depth. And the more we crumple up the paper, the closer to a solid our crumply object becomes. See what I mean?"

"Yes, I see that."

"In between that two-dimensional flat state and that three-dimensional 'infinitely crumply' state is a kind of 'in-between' state. In mathematics, which is what I study, we're very interested in those in-between states."

"But why?"

"Well, if there's an in-between state between zero and one dimension, and between one and two dimensions, and between two and three dimensions, we have to start wondering about what those states would look like when they have more than three dimensions—say more than three but less than four. What's in between?"

"I think all things are between there," offered Ceryl.

"Ah, but this crumply ball might have moved."

"Perhaps it was blown by the wind?"

"Sure. So, we have to think about how time affects things, too."

Ceryl looked thoughtfully at the crumpled ball of paper. "You know, we have a story about a great philosopher whose name was As Time. 'I am As Time,' he said. He taught the way of the two great truths—of the soul inside all things and in what is and what shall be."

As Time, the real As Time
Had a vision most sublime
Of the nature of space
In a glorious field
So was the essence of grace
In that vision revealed

As Time, today As Time
A philosopher's song writ in runic rhyme
Sails on rhapsodic seas
To an unknown shore
Hears it in the breeze
As it was before

As Time tomorrow flies
Faster than we realize
To ride a dark wave and sail a light breeze,
Find the truth of it all in a piece,
Raise up a dream in the hope it will fly—
At the end of it, l-o-v-e equals why

"Imagine we want to go somewhere. From here to there, maybe on a beach, somewhere nice like that, hmm?"

"I can see that," said Ceryl.

"This dot—this point—is our first footstep. And let's say we want to go in a very straight line. We mark a point here, and another over there and walk over there in a straight line, okay?"

"And of course, there's footprints on the way there. So, we'll make dots on our paper here to show that. And when we get there, we turn and come back. We make some more footprints. So, more dots. And if we go back and forth again, of course more footprints, right?"

"All these footprints they begin to appear between those two end-points, pretty soon you can start to see a line appearing. Going in one direction, we call that a 'one-dimensional' line. So that 'in-between' state, in between our first 'zero dimensional' point and that one-dimensional line, there's an in-between dimensional state. I want you to think about that."

"Now imagine we have made a straight line but in a different direction, going somewhere else. Now we have two dimensions. Now we have lines of footprints here and there, in more and more places until this two-dimensional space starts to fill up the whole beach with footprints. We'll draw that on our paper here, lots of crisscrossing lines."

"Now, there's another and another, all crisscrossing each other on this beach. Pretty soon, those footprints are almost everywhere in two dimensions. Okay?"

"Then we make another and another."

"It's the journey in all this. Everything that is."

"I think I'm not explaining it well. Sorry!"

"Now I draw another. And, in between those two, another and another, to show the gray zone between no-dimensionality and a singular point; of the nearly infinite lines that become the gray zone between one dimension and two; and of the infinitely crumpled two-dimensionality that crosses the line between 2-D and the solidness of the real world."

Susan wrote $Z_{n+1} = Z_n^2 + C$ in her book. "And some of us find ways to express ideas like these in our books."

"I cannot say in honesty I understand, but I hear that your story tells of the essential nature of all that is. And I believe you."

○ ○ ○

Susan found that one of the things she liked about listening to Ceryl's stories was the way they made her think and feel —not necessarily about the story, but about herself, her life.

Susan had been thinking a lot about the possible consequences of sending a message back in time. What if, she worried, sending that message created a causal chain that completely destroyed this future?

She imagined herself somewhere else, recounting tales from the world of the now, as a future that never was. What would she tell them? Would she say that long life is a valuable thing, or that time is a thief in all that it steals away? Would she warn all the migrants, the lost and the homeless, to beware of a future where they do not belong? Or teach them the lessons of this misappropriated god? Was this an oasis or a culture of fear, where the fairy tales are designed to keep children out of the pits?

Susan's eyes suddenly widened. The pits! "You talked about 'the pits' in that story. Have you *been* to one of these pits?"

The storyteller gave her a bemused look. "The pits? Those are only in stories we tell the children. Such stories are intended to teach a lesson—to keep them safe."

Kaedra heard Susan speaking and returned to the room to better understand what she was saying.

"But there really *are* people down there in what you call the pits," insisted Susan. "I've *been* down there."

"In fact, if you like, I'll take you there. I have to meet some friends tonight. They may need my assistance."

Kaedra shook her head. "But that is forbidden. There are no people there. Only monsters. And the all-consuming whirlwind. No one goes there. It's simply not allowed."

○ ○ ○

When the Council reconvened, Kaedra was called to speak about what she and the storyteller had learned from the travelers.

"The storyteller says they speak of a great destroyer of magic called 'science.' And how their vessel emerged from a whirlwind. They speak of the knowledge that all others grow old and die but they do not."

"And they say they have been to the underworld."

At this point, the murmurings in the chamber erupted into shouts. Members of the Assembly yelled and shook their fists at the Councillors. The Rhabdomancer banged his staff on the floor. The Chambermaster rolled his eyes and leaned close to the Chief Councillor, his voice barely audible over the pandemonium.

"It is just as the prophecy of the pale witch foretold."

"Order, order," cried the Chief Councillor, striking the podium repeatedly with the base of his chalice.

"Their story is that their entire belief system is based on the magical properties of a thing called 'science...'"

"It's some sort of quasi-religious infrastructure based on poppycock and dreams," sniffed the Chambermaster.

"They tell of a communication system—a shared vision—by which information about when other travelers in this magical whirlwind will appear. And they claim there are other beings elsewhere, in a place called 'the future' from which no one returns. These beings, it is said, are superior in both awareness and advancement. And yet, they know nothing of Anna!"

"How dare they? What nonsense! Let us pray to Anna."

"Find out where and when this whirlwind will appear next. And assemble a team to investigate these claims."

"Your Eminence. They have asked if they may be allowed to reenter the Temple of The Ancients. They say there are answers within."

"Indeed, there are. But I am dismayed to hear of their lack of faith in our beloved Anna. Allow them entry and watch closely, but do not interfere unless they try to damage the temple."

o o o

"The Advisory Committee has recommended that the High Council reconvene to provide a context for these findings, so that they may be assimilated into the Teachings."

The Assembly erupted in a storm of protest.

"So, these harbingers allege that our doctrine is flawed? How dare they?"

"Surely, the Council cannot allow such blasphemy! It's outrageous."

"They can't be serious. It's a sick joke."

"And what if these foolhards encourage others to believe in their wastrel ways?"

"I shall order the stories to remain untold," conceded the Chief Councillor.

"Did they give any indication that they were *dangerous*?"

"No, Chief Councillor," said Kaedra. "But they did want to show me something at the temple."

"Where are they now?"

"They are still at the Garden House Manor, excellency."

"Instruct the guards to fetch them from the manor. Kaedra, you will take them to the temple. Double the guard on all exits. We may yet discover how they managed to get into the temple undetected."

○ ○ ○

The guard arrived at the Chief Councillor's office quite breathless. "Sir," he puffed. "Kaedra and the travelers have vanished from the temple."

"Were there not guards watching all of the exits?"

"There were."

"Do not allow anyone in or out of the temple on my orders. They may still be inside."

○ ○ ○

Amir and Susan helped Kaedra down the elevator shaft

and through the hatch on the top of the elevator car. When at last all three of them stood in the elevator, Susan pointed to the table just outside the open door. "There's nothing to be afraid of. This is where my friends and I used to wor—." Just then, Kaedra saw the startlingly blue figure of Karl and nearly fell off the table.

"A monster!" she cried.

"It's okay, I'm used to it."

Surprisingly, Kaedra didn't ask many questions while she was there. But Amir was unusually chatty. He asked her about the structure of their government, why there weren't any machines around—and why weren't there any books? Where was all the technology?

She explained that The One was very old and very wise and had found that these were the paths to darkness. He had founded the Annatarian church and its teachings of the Virtuous Way. "We will surely be blessed if we follow him on the golden path to righteousness."

Their government was comprised of The Assembly and its Advisory Committee, the High Council and The Supreme Order. The Assembly, she said, was an elected body; the Council an appointed one. The Supreme Order, founded and led by The One himself, provided spiritual guidance for all.

The One seemed to be something of a mystery to everyone but her. She spoke of him reverently and said that he performed miracles and had lived for more than 400 years. It was said that he had seen the Great Fall with his own eyes and had fought the monsters of the underworld. The monsters and the evil ones were very real, she assured them. The Holy

Artefacts were proof. And then there were the prophecies. The One had foretold so much, Kaedra said, it was beyond doubt.

She did not tell them that he had foretold of their arrival as well.

○ ○ ○

Meanwhile...

"Have the pale witch and her accomplice been found yet?"

"No sir. We still do not know where they are. She was last seen entering the temple roughly two hours ago."

"Why were there not guards watching the temple?"

"There were."

"Did Kaedra say she gave any indication that she was planning to leave?"

"Not that we know of, Chief Councillor. Our sources indicate that she may have visited with a local Storyteller named Ceryl Wen earlier in the evening. We thought she was going to—"

The Chief Councillor interrupted. "Find that woman. Do not allow anyone in or out of the building and search the temple from top to bottom. They may still be inside."

○ ○ ○

17

The Dawn of the Second Great Age

Karl shone his flashlight over the main control console. "We have to get some power on down here before we do anything else. I can't work in the dark."

"Do you know where the electrical room is?"

"Yeah, it's down that corridor there, on the left side."

"I'll come with you."

"Nah, don't bother. I'll just be a minute."

Karl examined the power panel and the diagram above the switches on the panel. The breakers were labeled by section. The switches for the halls and rooms all the way down to the Annex were all on, except the ones for the lab. He toggled the broken circuits back on and heard Amir say "that's better!"

Karl returned to the control room and pointed to the desk console where Amir was sitting. "There should be a few more switches under that console, near your right knee—just open that door on the right side... Ya, that's it."

Under the other desk, Amir located the panel containing a second set of breakers. "Woo, this is interesting. Look at this! These ones look like they were deliberately turned off. I wonder why?"

Karl shone the light on the schematic diagram. "From the schematic, it looks like those are the switches for the field generators. Hey, and there's CA1. Ya, we need that one on. Check the panel under the next desk, will you?"

"These ones say SR1. They're all off," reported Amir.

"Okay, flip those six switches on."

Five LEDs lit up. "Well, that's better than nothing. Seems like they must have shut it down while it was at least partly operational."

"Not necessarily," said Karl. "The LEDs are probably just burnt out." He rapped on the panel. "Those things don't last forever. No biggie."

"So, do you think you can power up the system?"

"It's worth a try."

"Those two look like they're not getting power."

From underneath the main console, Karl said: "Just about ready...." He slid out from underneath the desk and closed the side panel doors. "When we get this thing rebooted," he said, "the first thing I want to do is to look at the logs to learn why it was powered down in the first place. These things are *supposed* to be completely failure-proof."

"If I were a betting man, I'd say 'multiple EMPs' was the most likely explanation for the kind of cascading failure scenario that might be capable of taking down a large number of redundant systems."

"Multiple EMPs would suggest either nukes or heavy-duty solar activity."

"Yeah, solar magnetic flares, maybe. Or maybe some kind of non-nuclear electromagnetic pulse weapon. Seems like a pretty plausible explanation for their nearly complete avoidance of electricity. Electricity Wars."

"I don't know. As we've just proven, there *is* electricity here, but they seem unaware of it. And the power seems to have been *deliberately* turned off. It seems like someone's got to be pulling the wool over these people's eyes. It's hard to imagine any other explanation."

"I'm still thinking there must have been some sort of war. I mean, how could there be no books? How can there be no machines? How could there be no U.S. government, no military, no civil infrastructure? It just doesn't make sense."

Well, one thing's for sure: we've gotta get out of crazy town to find out what's really going on. I strongly doubt that it's like this everywhere. And I'm going to find out."

"Well you know what I say?" smiled Karl, as he flipped a pair of light switches on the wall. "More power to you." The lights above the console flickered to life.

"Great! I wasn't sure if I should expect those to work. There should be some on the far wall, too."

A moment later, he had a working command-line open and was busily typing commands into it.

"All right, here we go." He lifted up the protective cover over the power button on the main panel and pressed the button. "Cross your fingers. It's rebooting now...."

"The system was down for how long?"

"We'll know in a few seconds," said Karl as the watched the commands flash by as the initialization sequence progressed.

A moment later, Karl had retrieved the logs. "Um, a little over 300 years since the last system event was recorded. Ha, that's George's code right there. See?"

"What's that one?" asked Li Yan. "Someone has made a lot of jumps—and ended up here. And look, they go way back. Whoa—way back, all the way to the original lab."

"Maybe it's the mysterious 'George Gomez.'"

"Really cool, by the way, that you made the logs list the departure location." Karl shrugged. "Oh, that's very old code. But ya, it works."

"The systems in this building have been inactive for hundreds of years—and now it's suddenly active again, right?"

"Yes. Actually, this panel covers the whole topside complex, I think. Several buildings in all."

Li Yan watched Susan trying to explain to Kaedra all that was going on. Kaedra was still completely awestruck by the fact that any of this was even here, practically right underneath their feet.

Li Yan approached Susan and smiled politely at Kaedra. "May I have a private word with you, please?"

Kaedra was clearly uncomfortable at what was going on around her. It was difficult to say what she imagined was happening when the AI speech systems came back online. She said nothing—but she looked shocked. "I'll be right back," Susan assured her.

Li Yan was wary of the potential impact. "The introduction of completely new technologies has always proven to be incredibly disruptive to those with a previously established way of life. In this case, we don't even know whether they *want* the power turned on."

"I agree, but it's not even that simple," replied Susan. "By all indications, these people thought our AI systems were the word of God. I feel like we're really messing with their culture. I mean, who are we to pull back the curtain and say 'look, there's no God—it's just a machine?'"

"You've gotta be kidding. They think the AI is a superior being that was silent for all this time as a test of their faith?"

Susan nodded. "And now it is making contact." She looked over at Kaedra, still mesmerized by the activity around her. Kaedra watched Karl with great interest as the blue monster-man's fingers flew over the console keyboard.

"I'm going to take her back up to the temple. I'm just not comfortable with throwing this huge variable into the equation without at least telling them what's going on." Amir heard them talking and came over to see if everything was okay.

"Yes, I'll come with you," Susan said to Kaedra. She then gave Amir a quick hug. "I'll try to reassure them that our technologies represent no threat."

"Once they see how the system can help them, they'll be grateful. We'll be heroes."

"Don't be so sure."

"Be careful."

"I will."

"Here, I'll give you a boost."

"Thanks."

"Up you go. Okay! Take care."

○ ○ ○

When Kaedra and Susan opened the door to the Chamber of the Council Building, the Chief Councillor was leading the Assembly in prayer.

"Lo, the time of the prophecy is at hand. Soon will come our day for rejoicing. May the patience of the faithful be justly rewarded. In Anna's name we pray. Amen."

Kaedra said, "I will speak to the Chambermaster. Have the coach take you to Wen Manor and ask Ceryl to find you a room, as my guest. I will see you there soon."

When Susan arrived at Wen Manor, Ceryl the Storyteller was sitting cross-legged on a pillow, as she often did, surrounded by a group of young teenagers. "This is a traditional story-song of the mythopoetic philosopher-king, In the Sun, who was a wizard of sound and light," she told them.

Time is always in the sun,
O wise and gracious one,
Lead us now from darkest night,
By thy eternal light.
Time is always in the sun,
Keeper of the day,
Preserveth thou our memories,
By the light of your true way.

"He heard the word...." The chants of her students echoed through the hall, sending shivers up the back of the storyteller's neck, as they always did when The Song was made real. The storyteller waved her hand to lead the class in the next set of verses.

> *He heard the word again made strong*
> *When carved into the dark.*
> *The current world was filled with song*
> *by the wizard of the park.*
> *And when he did ascend once more,*
> *he gave us sound and light*
> *and saw the journeys of before*
> *Illuminate the night.*

"And so it was...."

> *And so it was when in the sun*
> *brought from the skies above*
> *the sacred light; the holy spark*
> *of mercy, kindness, love.*

The storyteller continued in prose.

> *And his name is timeless, in the sun.*
> *He makes the paths connected.*
> *Time is all that's in the sun*
> *sees truth in light projected.*
> *In his eternal light we pray.*

Amen.

And when at last the Storyteller's story was told, it was almost dark. The time for singing and of telling was over.

"Did you enjoy the telling?" asked Ceryl, as she raised her yellow flag for the night. "Yes," replied Susan. "There's something familiar about that story."

"Yes, Timeless In The Sun touches us all."

Timeless In the Sun. The way Ceryl pronounced it suddenly jogged Susan's memory.

Of course.

"I *know* that story. He was known as the Wizard of Menlo Park."

o o o

Susan was curious. "Cer, what does the yellow flag mean?"

"That simply means my vessel is healthy. I fly that when I am feeling good. And you have made me feel really good today. Would you like to sleep with me?"

"Oh, gosh. That's very nice of you to offer. Maybe tomorrow."

Cer smiled coyly. "I don't know about tomorrow. Maybe the flag flies only today. But it's your decision, of course." She opened her arms invitingly and Susan gave her a warm hug.

"I bless you, goodnight."

"Thank you for your kindness."

o o o

Awake

Amir was nodding off. Karl was still working at the main control console.

"Hey, where's Li Yan?"

"Somewhere around here," said Amir sleepily. "She said she was going to make a map of the place. So, I dunno where she is, exactly."

"Want an energy bar?"

"Yeah, sure," Amir said with a yawn. "Thanks."

"Have you decided when you're leaving crazy town—or where you'll go?"

"No, not yet. I wanted to ask Susan if she'll come with me."

"You like her, don't you?"

"Oh yeah, sure. Oh, you mean like a girlfriend? Nah, she's not interested."

"Oh, I wouldn't be so sure. By the way, did you know how to track the jumps from a specific jump-point?"

"No! You know how to do that?"

"Oh, sure. That's how Li Yan and I followed George here. It's not the most user-friendly notation system—even after all this time! —but it's reliable." Karl stopped typing and turned to face Amir. "Hey, when you were starting out, did you have other people sending you supplies at specified times?"

"No. Good idea, though."

"I had a friend on the original team who sent me a lot of stuff over the years. They never knew about her. She stayed on the project right through to retirement, so she was a good source. I have all the manuals stored on here."

"Yeah, we had a fairly good system going where we would leave requests for other jumpers to bring us supplies: books and pens and whatnot. Just after you guys left—I wasn't there at that point, as I recall—the company set up a supply program where you could schedule stuff to be sent to you at particular times. As long as you were there when it arrived and you could show the right ID, you could pick it up."

"They stopped doing that around year three, I heard. But not my gal—she just kept right on sending stuff."

He turned back to his screen and scrolled through the code he had just written. "We got kinda fancy for a while. I got them to send fuel cells and various gadgets. Even an electric bike! But I traveled pretty light after that. I got robbed a couple of times."

"How did you manage to get into the program if they were suing you?"

"Heh heh. My friend got me through the door on his card. I carried fake ID. And a pretty lame disguise. For-tunately, they weren't too strict after they started allowing social-service exemptions. I used to have a couple of pieces of decent-looking photo ID, altered just enough so that the facial recognition systems wouldn't find a match...."

"A1 was the area at the end of that really long corridor, right?"

"Yeah, Rössler took me over there when I started there."

"Yeah, me too. What was that server farm area called, again?"

"I think it was SR1—something like that. It was near The Annex, right?"

"Yes, that's it. I think maybe we should go over there."

"It was really far, like a kilometer away or something. We took a vehicle."

"Well, it's highly unlikely there will be any working vehicles up at this end of the building. But if there were, we could probably plug it in now, at least. In any case, I'm up for a long walk. We've got food and water. The lights are on. Seems doable."

"Omigod. Those tire marks. I swear those are from my old electric motorbike—the one that got stolen. Motherf—...."

"Shh! Listen." The faint sounds of machinery could be heard echoing in the corridor.

Karl was walking ahead when he suddenly slid behind one of the tall posts on the nearest side of the hall and gestured silently to Amir. Someone—or something—was coming down the hall. They could hear the hum of motors and a hushed symphony of tiny clicks and clacks, wheezes and whirs. A vaguely humanoid utility bot robot stepped out of the equipment bay area's charging station.

It stopped all movement for a second, then swiveled its metallic head in Karl's direction.

"Halt! Identify yourself." Amir froze.

Karl put his finger to his lips and shook his head.

Two more bots—much more advanced security bot models, this time—approached from behind them, heading directly for them.

"*Scheisse.*"

The bots addressed Amir and Karl.

"This is a restricted area. Please come with us. You will not be harmed if you do not resist. Thank you for your cooperation."

Karl made a run for the hallway.

With astonishing speed, the security bot intercepted him and pointed a Taser at him.

"Surrender immediately or risk prosecution and possible injury," it intoned, in a markedly more authoritarian voice. "Security personnel have been alerted. All exits are monitored."

"Come on, man, let's just go with them. I don't wanna get shot."

The utility bot followed behind Karl and Amir as the security bots led them down the corridor.

"I wonder why these bots are roaming around down here," whispered Karl. "They seem way more advanced than anything we've seen before." Karl glanced at the utility bot trailing him. Well, maybe not *that* one."

The security bots came to a stop in front of a pair of

metallic doors. "This used to be where George worked," Karl noted in a hushed voice.

Amir was mute. He looked worried. The bot pointed to the screen and said "Remain here. A service representative will speak with you momentarily. Thank you for your patience." The bot then turned and stationed itself at the far side of the doorway.

A voice crackled through the sound system. "Welcome, travelers. You look like you might need assistance. How can we help?"

Karl looked around for a security camera, trying not to be too obvious about it.

"We are here because we urgently need to contact someone in charge," said Amir. "We wish to share information of the utmost importance with your government."

"You may speak now. Your concerns will be noted."

"No, no. We need to speak to whoever is in charge here. It is extremely urgent that we speak to—"

"Amir Frede Roy," said the voice, interrupting. "Are you now or have you ever been an intern or contract employee of the company formerly known as Andna Corporation?"

Amir nodded, then realized a voice response was probably necessary. "Yes?"

"Thank you for your response, Amir," said the voice. It seemed oddly familiar.

"And you, Karl Otto Schraeder..." The spatial position of the audio noticeably shifted from Amir to where Karl was standing. "Are you now or have you ever been a full-time or contract employee of the company formerly known as Andna Corporation?"

"No, my name is Horst Schtickler," fibbed Karl. Amir glared at him.

"As you wish, *Horst.*"

"Yes, that's me. You wanna see my ID? And how about answering my question?"

"Horst Schtickler, are you now or have you ever been a self-employed laborer in Toms River, New Jersey?"

"It's totally ignoring my requests now," said Karl, mildly amused that it was quoting his fake résumé.

Karl could barely conceal his contempt. "Whatever. Yes, that's me. We need to speak someone in charge. *Now.*"

"You've got mail," said the voice. "I have a message here from Li Yan Zhang. Would you like to accept it?"

"Ya, ya," he muttered in exasperation. A second later, Li Yan's familiar voice was heard.

"Hey K,

If you're hearing this message, it means I finally found you. George sends his best regards. You'll be happy to know that his lawsuit was finally settled. It was in the circuit courts for 14 years! See you soon.

L."

--End of message--

"Oh, that's an old one. That was just before George jumped here."

--Next message--

"There is a private message from you from Rhonda. Will you accept the message?"

"Uh, can I take that privately somewhere?"

A different number in large type appeared on each of the displays in the room. "Please specify the display upon which you wish to read this private message."

Karl selected the closest screen. "#1," he said, and tapped it for good measure.

A video with captions appeared. "Carrie is graduating next month, so we're kind of busy with that. Well, hope you are well. Carrie says hi. Bye Karl. Thanks again for everything you've done for us. Call me sometime."

--End of message--

"That was my old girlfriend," he explained to Amir. "Honestly, I wasn't sure that was suitable for all ears, if you know what I mean, ha."

Just then they heard a thump and an echoing voice coming from outside the room:

"Greetings, Susan Alice Everett of Trenton, New Jersey. Are you now or have you ever been a full-time or contract employee of the company formerly known as Andna Corporation?"

Amir opened the door and looked down the corridor. "Susan! How nice of you to drop in."

"Your response is required," said the system.

Karl stuck his head out of the room. "That's our new friend, the robot interrogator and old-timey email courier."

"I brought some food."

"That is an invalid response."

"Screw that thing," said Susan, handing an apple to each of them.

"Fantastic. I'm really tired of energy bars."

"You've still got drinking water?"

"Yeah."

"Well, that's good. I thought I'd better see what you night owls were up to."

"Ya, I really should get some sleep one of these days, ha!"

"Where were you?"

"I got to know one of the Storytellers and she showed me around a bit. They haven't got any electric lights up there and everyone there was bedding down for the evening, so…"

"Yeah," said Amir, "I guess we've got to find a place where you can wash up and sleep, too."

"Your response is—"

"Excuse me, whoever the *fuck* you are," Susan interrupted. "Could we meet with you face to face?"

A handsome man's face appeared on the video screen.

"You can call me Xavier," said the face. It sounded exactly like George.

"Is that you, George?"

"It's a bot, I think," whispered Amir.

"Please call me Xavier. Do you have any questions?" asked Xavier.

Concerned that the bot might simply be using the question as a way of extracting a 'yes' answer for its file, Susan remained cagey. "Well, Xavier, to be honest, I'm a little confused. What are you?"

"I am your host for this tour. Would you prefer to select a different tour guide?"

Karl peered at the display screen. It was hard to tell for sure....

"Xavier, are you a chatbot?"

"I'm impressed with your powers of observation and/or deduction," said the figure on the screen. "Indeed, I am an agent here to assist *you*—our guests."

"Xavier, I don't mean to be rude, but where we come from, it is customary for hosts to meet their guests in person. Would you agree with that statement, Amir?"

"Yes, yes I would," stammered Amir, as he studied Xavier's on-screen avatar.

"Can we meet the Xavier in person?"

"Yes. Please wait here. Xavier is on his way. It was my pleasure to assist you. Goodbye."

Portions of the clear glass walls of the office suddenly became opaque and an animated set of doors suddenly opened, *Star Trek* style. Through them emerged what looked like a holographic movie of their friend George. The hologram waved in their direction. "Greetings, travelers," it said in George's voice.

"Okay, that is creepy," said Karl.

It occurred to Amir that the figure's eyes didn't look quite right when they blinked. There was a hint of 'uncanny valley' there. And that skin....

"This is bullshit," grumbled Karl, taking off his reading glasses. "Okay, no more holograms, no more videos. Is real George available? Can we talk to a real person, please?"

"I can see you have many questions," said the movie of

George. "Would you like me to show you around a bit? You can follow me from wall..."

The hologram walked from one panel to the next. "...to wall, or from screen..." The figure vanished and the face reappeared on the nearest monitor.

"...to screen, like this. Do you want to take a tour?"

"Omigod," said Amir, "it's a filthy marketing bot that looks like George."

Susan just shook her head. "I can't think of anything less George-like than this."

"I'd like to take the tour, actually," said Karl, intrigued. "Okay, you crazy bot, let's do it. Give us the tour back to CA1."

"Good choice. We can begin your tour as soon as you're ready. To begin, just say 'Begin the tour.'"

"Okay, okay—ready?" asked Karl, with mock—or maybe real—enthusiasm.

Amir nodded. Susan shrugged.

"Begin the tour."

"This area is known as Ops station alpha," said the hologram of George. "Please, follow me." The image of George flashed to the glass wall on the opposite side of the hallway. "This way, please. Follow me!"

As they walked, the system's cameras monitored their body language and eye movements, tracked their locations and listened for questions.

"I know you are wondering why I look like your friend," said the hologram of George. The eye trackers detected that this caught the attention of both Amir and Karl.

"Yeah, about that," said Karl. "I think we'll just call you George from now on."

Hologram George smiled. "You can call me anytime. I'm here to help travelers feel more at ease by having a familiar person or pet introduce them to their new environment. If you would rather change the tour guide, just say 'change the tour guide.'"

Karl laughed out loud. "A pet!? I've gotta see this. Change the tour guide."

The tour guide's physical form, identity and persona began to cycle through various choices—young and old, thin and fat, females, furries, you name it. There was even a blue one.

"Oh, for god's sake. Let's have the furry one."

"We welcome travelers of all nationalities, religions, ages and genders. You'll meet some of your fellow travelers soon. The most important thing I have to share with you," said Hologram George, now with furry ears and a tail, "is to assure you that we have your very best interests in mind. Job fairs, career training, and a full range of social services are available upon request...."

o o o

19

Bad Bits and Bots

"George, George. Can you stop, please? I like what I'm hearing about all these wonderful social services you *say* you provide, but I'm just not *seeing* them. I mean, we just want to send an urgent message to someone in charge. Can you help us with that?"

"I am sorry. Your group's status as *contractor* does not allow for that level of communication."

"Do you wish to leave a message in the general mailbox?"

"Ah, why not. Ya, I want to leave a message."

"Say 'Save Message' or 'I need help' at any time, or say 'Send message' when you are ready to send. Please begin dictating your message now."

"This is an urgent message for whoever is in charge of the Aeronautics/Space-Time Research project responsible for the NASA invention that allowed communications via entangled status bits. Refer to NASA code 2038119-Karl Schraeder to prove that we are who we say we are."

"Send Message."

"And have them CC Amir and Susan on any replies."

"I am sorry. Your group's status as *contractor* does not allow for that level of communication."

"Oh really? But our group's status is high enough that you chase us around with friggin' robots?"

"What robots?" Susan quietly asked Amir.

"Bad ones," whispered Amir, tersely.

"Please note: one of those robots was not ours, and that's why we sent out our own security bots. This bot arrived on platform CA1 approximately 22 minutes ago and belong to Karl Schraeder. Please remember: we are not responsible for your personal property."

Amir looked at Karl, surprised.

"Well, I think the *other* robots came on a bit strong," said Amir, scowling. "They pointed guns at us and were quite threatening."

"Unnecessarily scary."

"On behalf of Andna LLC, please accept our apologies for any issues you may encounter in our programming services. Your safety and well-being are important to us. Our service bots are fully self-optimizing and designed to respond in the method most likely to produce the optimal result—which, in this case, is to ensure your safety."

"Ya, I can see how that self-optimizing programming is working out for you."

Oh, he's put his foot in it now, thought Amir. "Shh!"

"Okay, here's a question for you, my furry friend: have any

of the people upstairs in that so-called 'temple' ever accessed your systems?"

"I am sorry. Your group's status as *contractor* does not allow for that level of disclosure."

"Aha! Now we're getting somewhere. Okay, use security authorization override code 2038119-George Gunderson."

"If you asked, 'have any of the people upstairs ever accessed your systems,' please say 'continue.' If you want to ask a different question, just say 'I have a different question.'"

"Ugh, who programmed this?" Karl grumbled. "Oh, wait, wait. 'Continue.'"

"The answer to your question is *yes*. There have been *two* users who fit that description. 'Name not available' and 'George Gunderson.'"

"Hmm. Can you display a full list of the activities of user 'Name not available' on the screen here?"

"One moment please."

"Aha. Look, there's an unexpected power-down command. Whoever this is, he or she doesn't know how to shut the system down properly. So that pretty much exonerates George."

Karl noticed the list contained a very large number of jumps, and a nearly equal volume of status messages sent. Interesting.

"Okay, locate user 'George Gunderson.'"

"George Gunderson is in Server Room SR1."

"Wha—?!"

"Would you like to speak with him?"

"Yes."

"George—it's Karl!"

"Hey there Karl. How are ya, buddy?"

"Great. Man, we've been looking for you for *ages*. Literally ages. I'm here with Susan and Amir. And Li Yan is around here, too. Hey, do you have any contact with the people upstairs in the temple?"

"No, but I used to. They have chosen to renounce technology in all respects. They have their own beliefs and customs, and I respect that."

"Down here, however, we embrace technology and believe in the potential for enhancement of the self in all its forms. We celebrate diversity here. Come, let me show you around—a bit."

"You can see us right now?" asked Amir.

"Uh huh, almost everywhere," replied George. "Everywhere that matters, one might argue. We're very data-driven here, you'll see. We evaluate risks as we do paths and probabilities. May I tell you a little more about the robot that followed you?"

"Yes," said Amir. Karl looked nonplussed. And Susan was downright suspicious. This *looked and sounded* like George, but didn't *speak* like him.

"It is, we would imagine, unfamiliar to you. It was designed about 40 years ago as a tracker bot. When it arrived, we ran a detailed analysis on it to better understand its purpose. What we discovered was interesting: it was not sent from your time, although it contains information from that period."

"That *is* interesting."

"It also contained a great deal of information about its predecessors."

"Now, we have records of various other types of packages arriving over the past couple of centuries. At first, we received data in various digital formats. These were a compatibility nightmare. In as little as 40 or 50 years, it became virtually impossible to connect the storage devices and read the data formats. We received tablets, disks, optical media—at one point, they were even sending books. It was very labor-intensive for us to physically hook up various oddball electrical connectors. And the 'standards' kept changing!"

"As it turns out, the information was repackaged and expanded upon numerous times since the first information packets started arriving via the machine."

"As far as we can tell, the original transmissions were relatively simple. We received several small tablets containing videos, texts and small-scale data repositories. These were sent by your scientists and project leaders, in efforts to help travelers like yourselves with social services, non-expiring ID packages, and other information. We imagine that they must sent out many such devices to all time periods in which jumpers had landed."

"However, as time went on and additional information became relevant to your welfare, these devices, we surmise, began to seem inadequate for the tasks."

"And then, as time went by, unfortunately, the frequency with which these packages arrived decreased to nearly nothing. (And, when you consider the math, it's really not surprising.)"

"So, we were a bit surprised when this robot appeared. At some point no more than 40 years ago, they apparently decided to upgrade the delivery systems to one or more of these tracker bots."

"It's a heuristic system that automatically updates its data formats and it tracks based on probability. It's certainly a much better system than those old tablets, many of which were very limited in their geographical and temporal logging capabilities."

"This bot, for example, had jumped three times before it arrived here. It contains records of several hundred participants in the Andna Corporation and Andna LLC time-jumping programs, and has updated records of all those it has found to date. Some of course, add their own messages and pass them on, with notices of births, deaths, marriages, and so on."

"It was sent here specifically to track the whereabouts of travelers and pass on messages from your time to ours."

"And it seems to have worked pretty well," said Amir. "It found us."

"And the people up in the temple," Karl asked George, "were you helping them to time-travel?"

"Yes, and we sent some messages too. But I got wise to their game and I'm done with that now."

"Ya, sending messages is something I've been working on, too. Have you got the code from NASA that sends messages backwards in time?"

"And most importantly," Amir added, "have you discovered how to *travel* backwards in time?"

"Both questions have short and long answers—and both answers are similar. The short answer to both is 'no.'"

"With that said, we have analyzed a great deal of data from time-jumpers and have found that the risk-to-reward ratio does not favor the escapists. Those who encounter serious issues may—or may not—find an elusive answer or solution more readily by jumping forward—and in such cases, traveling just far enough to hit the cusp of innovation presents the ideal business scenario. But generally, we have not found this to be a reliable course of action. As a consequence, we continue to offer selected individuals the freedom to jump forward, but as the vast majority has already shown a preference not to, we no longer offer escapism as a solution to the general populace."

"We are particularly interested in anything you can tell us about entangled qubit communications," said Susan. "Can you assist us with that?"

"That would be the long answer."

"Your request for a detailed answer has been noted. While you are waiting, we would be very interested in your help in filling in missing pieces in our history. Any contributions you can share, we would be most grateful to receive."

"In exchange, we can offer you access to some of our own technology. Welcome to *your* future!" George smiled graciously. "Pardon me; I must step away to take care of something. I will return momentarily."

The door opening animation ran again and George entered the holographic doorway and was gone.

"That sure as hell isn't the George I know," declared Susan. "Either it's a bot, or he's taken one hell of a marketing class."

Karl's manner immediately changed. "I agree with Susan. I'm pretty sure that's not our George."

"That's weird," said Amir. "Why would the system have a virtual tour guide that looks like George, and another bot that *also* pretends to be him?"

"And why does a bot have to go off to take care of something else?"

"Simple answer: it doesn't," said Karl.

When George blinked back onto the screen, Susan, Amir and Karl were gone.

A status report appeared on the console display. "A low-level command override has recently been deployed in this area. The records show an individual by the name of Horst Schtickler using an ID associated with Karl Schraeder initiated accelerator activity lasting 28.4 seconds approximately four minutes ago using a forged identity."

An executive command was automatically issued to the security bots and they immediately began sweeping the area.

○ ○ ○

Karl typed commands into a local terminal. "Okay. I've turned off all the motion detectors and cameras in this area. I think that should hide our tracks for a while."

"How did you—?"

"When we first got here—remember, before the bots arrived, when we first powered up the system? —I had a few minutes at a console and managed to give myself root access using—believe it or not—George's old backdoor codes. Those codes only worked on a local terminal, so I guess the AI never saw them as a threat. Or, who knows, maybe it's still crappier at basic security administration than your typical IT amateur."

"Shhh. Just a moment," whispered Susan. She put her finger to her lips and pointed to the elevator shaft.

"Maybe it's Li Yan," whispered Amir.

Susan shook her head. Nope. This was loud—almost comically loud, like the sounds of several very clumsy people, or someone trying to be as noisy as humanly possible.

"What the *hell* is that?"

"Not Li Yan, I'm guessing."

"We better get out of here." Karl was typing furiously. "Is everybody ready to jump?" he whispered. "I'll be ready in about 15 seconds. Stand over there on the jump platform." There was no time for a pod.

"Field integrity at 80%."

"10 seconds..."

90%! He backed away from the console and headed toward the jump platform.

Just then, two guards from the temple upstairs forced open the elevator door and dropped noisily onto the control room floor. A third was close behind.

"Stay there!" shouted Karl. "5 seconds till the jump."

"Watch out Karl!" shouted Susan, as the temple guards lunged toward him.

And they were gone.

○ ○ ○

25 minutes and 59 seconds later....

Susan had seen it before: Amir was going to pieces again. "Now everybody's after us!" he moaned.

"Can't say I disagree with ya, pal," said Karl. "It's really not safe to stay here anymore."

"But, but... Where will we go?"

"I dunno. But I've been thinking: all those people at the wrap party all exited at the far end of the complex, where we've never been. I think chances are pretty good that we'll find an exit out that way, and maybe even people who can help us. Anyway, I just want to get as far away from crazy town as possible."

"What about Li Yan?"

"She'll find us. She always does."

20

The Restoration

The three guards stood in the side of the Chambermaster's desk. "What is it?" he asked impatiently.

"The Chief Councillor sent us, sir," said one.

"Well, come on—tell me your news, then," he commanded.

"Sir, we witnessed a miracle. The pale witch, and two others...*vanished* in the magical whirlwind."

"You're *sure*? What exactly did you see?"

"It was just as the prophecies *said*. A cyclonic wind arose without warning—"

"Where there could be no such wind," interjected the other— "and they just *disappeared*."

"I saw it too, sir," said the third.

"Where exactly was this?" asked the Chambermaster.

"We discovered—actually *he* discovered—a hidden doorway behind one of the tapestries in the temple."

"Unbelievable," said the Chambermaster.

"It's true, sir. And we climbed down very far until at last

we found a magical place with lights and wonderous things beyond belief."

"We saw a monster, too," said the third.

The Chambermaster put his hand on his forehead. "You found a door ... to the *underworld*, and encountered a *monster*, right underneath the *temple*? It's unbelievable."

"It's all true sir."

"This is truly ... uh, worthy of The One's attention ... and consideration. Wait here!"

"Your Eminence, there are three guards here who, uh, have witnessed something quite miraculous. I promise you: you'll want to hear what they have to say."

The One waved his wizened hand. "Send them in."

o o o

Susan peered at the terminal where Karl had been working. "Before we go, I want us to learn as much as possible from the New History records and whatever other sources are available. Especially if we end up having to hunt or forage for food or shelter out there, we need to know what the hell we're up against. All those stories of monsters and 'evil ones' have got me a bit nervous, to be honest."

"Me too," admitted Amir.

"I'm dumping the data to this tablet, so we'll all be able to read it," said Karl. "I've left a message for Li Yan, too, in case she gets one of those old-timey email notifications from the system here, like we did."

"Jeez, I dunno," whinged Amir. "Don't you think George or whoever that was could help us? He must have somewhere to stay and food to eat? They *did* say our safety and well-being was a priority."

"Sorry pal, I don't trust either of those bots. But you're welcome to stay if you think you'll be okay."

"I actually do have a place to stay up there," noted Susan. " I could ask them if they can make accommodations for you guys and Li Yan."

"*If* we find her."

"We'll find her. Stop worrying."

"We're not even sure we can get past the *guards* up there, Susan. In fact, I think it's very likely I, being a person of color, *won't* get past them."

"All right, look: Li Yan is down here somewhere and I'm getting a little concerned that she hasn't made it back yet. I'm going to try to find her. If anyone wants to join me on what might end up being a rescue mission, you're welcome to. If *you* guys find her before I do, tell her that I've gone out to area A1 looking for her. And I dunno, if there's a place for you two up there in the temple, that's great, and I wish you all the best. I'm gonna try and find Li and then stick to the original plan: to find George. God, I thought we'd really found him there for a while."

"Well, I'm going to climb up to the temple and let them know I'm okay. I made some friends up there and they're probably worried about me. But you know what? If it doesn't work out, I'll find you; I'll catch up with you. I'm going to leave this food with you guys. There's a couple more apples, some bread and those weird-looking things that taste like coconut. They're pretty hard to open, unfortunately."

"That's okay. We have a pod full of tools right over there. Thanks a lot!"

"Hey, what if we all leave messages for each other on the wall outside the L106 Big Room here? You know, where we had the briefing session and the wrap party. What do you think?"

"Ya, I like it."

"I'll look there to find out where you guys are, okay?"

"That sounds like a plan. Okay Susan—good luck!"

"What about you, Amir?"

"I ... I feel like I have some more questions that the tour guide guy could probably answer. I was thinking of stopping in there for a few minutes."

"Knock yourself out. Tell ya what: I'll be here for 15 more minutes or so. If you're back here by the time I'm ready to leave, we'll go together. If not, just catch up when you can. And use that message system Susan mentioned. That's a good idea."

Amir looked at the food on the table. "Actually, maybe I'll just eat a little bit before I go. I'm pretty hungry."

"Ya, me too." They each tore off a piece from the loaf of bread and sat silently eating it for a moment. Karl scrolled through articles in the New Historians project database.

"Hey, look at this article here. From 300 years ago—can you believe it?"

"Whoa—This article says that XAVR—remember our old AI system at MPAX?—gained popularity with investors and attracted $4.2 billion in venture capital funding after it outperformed several competitors in successfully fending off an initial wave of global cyber-attacks. But investors pulled out *en masse* after its host systems were damaged in a second-wave attack."

"Was that the nutjob guy with the van full of explosives?"

"I think they're referring to the transit pod full of bombs. Or maybe both. Interestingly, all references to time travel seem to have been redacted from these documents."

"Apparently, they burned through all the money and were going to shut XAVR down. And that's when the military stepped in. They helped broker the deal with NASA that led to Andna LLC and saved the company. Ah, and they re-named XAVR to Ada—ostensibly an acronym for 'Advanced Defensive Analytics.'"

"Yeah, right."

"Oops! They discovered Ada's database had been cor-rupted; large sections had been lost. And at that point, some-body shut it down completely. Ada went silent."

"And then came all that stuff we've heard about: Lawsuits, Stern got ousted, bankruptcy, blah bla."

"Hm, this apparently all happened at the beginning of the period now known as the Great Fall: It says terrorists attacked *all* of the big superpowers with EMP weapons powerful enough to damage even milspec-hardened devices. At first, the agencies thought they were just determined hackers. How-ever, all the signs suggested these were state-sponsored attacks. This sparked a wave of warfare that took down numerous other electronic systems around the globe."

"When was this? I think we might have jumped into a period just before that. Things were very tense; the news media were talking about global conflicts on an unprecedented scale."

"That was about three hundred years ago—the period before the restoration began. It says here the U.S. government did a big restructuring effort when DC became the 51st state, and then Hawaii announced that it wanted to become a commonwealth. Puerto Rico, meanwhile, voted 91 percent in favor of becoming a state *instead* of a commonwealth. California had a big referendum on whether they should become a separate country. And then Texas and most of the other 'stripe states' in middle America decided they didn't want to be 'united states' any more, and that led to ... well, it sounds pretty chaotic. Religious fanatics took it to be the apocalypse and, several generations later, the stories of an all-knowing omniscient being that guided the development of humanity became the stuff of myth and—at least in this part of the world—the foundation for the Annatarian religion."

"This period became known as The Restoration. Their descendants, it says here, took it as an opportunity to integrate and take control of all of the interconnected AI systems, first on a national level and, soon thereafter, globally." He read through the article. "Oh, this is freaky: it says there's a cult of 'Sternists,' radical activists inspired by Isaac Stern who call him a hero."

"What the—?"

"The big innovation that occurred during this period of restoration was the development of expanded intelligence in humans. The integration of AI-based intelligence and awareness introduced a level of capability that, it says here, *left the non-augmented populace far behind."*

"Freaky," said Amir under his breath.

"Oh, here's a reference to time-jumping that's *not* redacted. Interesting... A great many of the early pioneers in expanded intelligence programs were time-jumpers, who originally used these technologies to 'catch up' with the advancements of a more advanced society.

"They were eager early adopters of augmented intelligence technologies, bla bla bla..." He skipped ahead. "These systems allowed the automatic integration of intelligence-enhancing bio-mods that went far beyond anything humans had been previously able to achieve."

"Hmm. Interesting," he mumbled as he continued reading. "Here's a good quote: This new capability soon led to a schism between the 'augmented' and 'unenlightened' populations that widened as we left them behind. And—this is hilarious—the guy being interviewed says: 'unfortunately, I can't fully explain or demonstrate that to you, as you are both *un*augmented.'"

"*Phhtt*. And how does one get 'augmented?'"

"It says it's an automated procedure. It's interesting: the article calls it 'the mother program' that provided their forefathers with a genetic program that augments embryos at birth. But these remarkable children developed a retrovirus-and-nanotech solution that could upgrade mature brains 'in place,' so to speak. And get this: Retroviral or at-birth augmentation is considered a *prerequisite* for meaningful employment these days. *What?!*"

"So, what—do these jokers just plug straight into the AI or something like that?"

"It doesn't sound like it," replied Karl. "They claim they are really just—and I quote—'broadening the scope of comprehension by a few orders of magnitude.' More than anything, it just allows humans to keep up with the AI."

"I don't like the way all that crap's marketed," grumbled Susan.

"Huh. They call these augmented people 'humana;' the anti-augmentation advocates call themselves 'human,' of course—and then there's me in the blue and the monsters."

"And all the migrants—and the jumpers. Are they in or are they out?"

"I don't want to be *in* on that. That turns me off—completely."

"Have you had enough to eat? I'm going to go now. Do you want any of this food?"

"Maybe just an apple, thanks."

Karl packed up his tablet and the remaining food in a backpack and slung it over his shoulder.

"See you later."

"Okay, bye."

o   o   o

152 meters to the Security Checkpoint said a sign, its sticker covering the old measurement in feet now peeling at the edges. Not a good first impression, thought Karl.

As he walked down the hall to the part of the building where the big meeting room was, the number of signs increased. *Show your Transit Pass and Picture ID at the Security Checkpoint* said one. *You must complete all Security Checks before entering the Arrival Lounge,* said another. *Physical violence, threatening behavior or abusive language will not be tolerated* said a third. Karl walked by the security cameras and the now-dark observation windows where, in earlier times, incoming travelers had been 'pre-screened' and known criminals, suspected terrorists, and other potential troublemakers ID'ed by the facility's facial recognition and profiling systems. But no more.

When Karl got to the plate-glass door of the Arrival Lounge, it was dark inside. He rattled the door anyway. It was locked.

On the glass panel next to the door, the figure of Hologram George flickered to life. "Not you again," grumbled Karl.

"Hey buddy," said Hologram George. "Where are you off to?"

"You know, I'm really not in the mood to talk to a bot, unless you can tell me where Li Yan Zhang is."

"No problem," said Hologram George. "Just a moment while I look for her. This is her, right?" A rectangular video of Li Yan lying motionless on the ground appeared.

"Omigod. Where is that image coming from?"

"That image is displaying the view from 848 meters east of your present location. Would you like me to lead you there?"

"Yes!" shouted Karl. He pulled the backpack a little higher on his shoulders and began to run. The figure of George walked from panel to panel, somehow keeping up with him as he ran.

"So," said Hologram George. "Are you and Li Yan a couple?" That seemed to Karl as an oddly inappropriate question for a chatbot—even a filthy marketing bot like this one—to be asking.

Panting, Karl stopped to catch his breath. "What the hell kind of question is that? It's none of your goddamned business."

"Sorry, man, I just thought that, you know, as old friends, you might want to tell me about something like that. No offense intended. I was just wondering."

"Old friends?"

"Uh, yeah. We've shared a few friendly secrets over the years, haven't we? I told you all about my lawsuit, didn't I? And Li Yan told you that that lawsuit took 14 years to settle, right? A bot wouldn't know that, would it?"

"It might," said Karl, beginning to jog again.

The hologram wasn't running but kept up—the animated image on the translucent wall panels rather disconcertingly just floated alongside Karl as he ran. "All right. Here's one: you met Andrea the intern, *right?* I went *out* with her. Hell, I would have *stayed* there with her if they hadn't kicked me out. A bot wouldn't say *that*, would it? We're not exactly *strangers* here, Karl."

Jesus, it *is* George, realized Karl.

"Well then, what the hell are you doing here as a hologram? I've been looking for you for ages."

"Indeed, you have. I apologize for not greeting you personally when we first interacted. That was my agent, taking care of names I don't recognize, eh, *Horst Schtickler?* Was it you who turned the power on?"

"It may have been," bluffed Karl, recalling that Amir did most of the switch-flipping.

"Well, thank you for that. Going black when the power goes off is horrible, let me tell you."

The animation came to a standstill just ahead of Karl. "You are approaching Li Yan's location."

Karl ran over to Li Yan and raised her wrist to feel for a pulse. She immediately grabbed his arm and very nearly broke it.

"Whoa, whoa! Just seeing if you are all right. I thought you were—"

"I was just taking a nap. Hey, have you got any food?"

"Ya, right here." He opened the bag and gave her an apple. "I'm so glad you're okay. We were getting worried."

"Where's Amir and Susan?" she said, biting into the apple.

"Amir stayed behind—ironically, to talk with this guy here..." He pointed to Hologram George. "...but I dunno about Susan. She has a place to stay up there in, you know, crazy town. The church cult or whatever it is. They are strange. She's not far away, though. By the way, how did the mapping go?"

"Fantastic," she said, taking a bite of the apple. "Mm, so good. I've got a pretty good drawing of the whole place, more or less to scale. Man, this complex is big. A lot of the doors are locked, unfortunately."

"Hey, did you ever make it outside?"

"Yes, I did. In fact, I walked all the around the complex to get a feel for the surrounding area."

"See anything interesting?"

"Two words: fish people. These cross-species hybrids are freaky as hell. But they seem nice. And it's not all like that place upstairs."

In fact, there was a vibrant community of people and hybridized humanoids with various types of Managed DNA throughout the neighborhood. The area to the east of the temple was still a small town, not that much different than you might expect a small town in the 25th century to be. These days, most everyone outside the old cities just got along.

"So," said Li Yan in between bites of her apple, "I have to ask: Why is there a hologram of George here?"

"Actually, it was Amir that explained things to me," said George.

"Funnily enough, I had a notification set to trigger if 'Karl Otto Schraeder' or his picture ID came through security. But our man here used *fake* ID and I just wasn't expecting that."

"My bad. I had to get through the checkpoint somehow, though."

"As for why I'm here, well, there *was*—and apparently still *is*—a program whereby people could do the intelligence augmentation procedure. So, I did that. Very cool. Really did a lot for my self-esteem and my coding chops. And chicks dig super-smart guys. Who knew?"

"Oh dear," said Li Yan, rolling her eyes in Karl's direction.

"Anyway, the augmentation was a service offered by the training department here, as it increases the career path viability and general employability of those who get the procedure done. But there was this other option called Virtualization that really intrigued me. I couldn't afford it, though. And then I found out about this option where, if you let them use your virtual entity part of the time for marketing purposes, it becomes free."

"Bingo," said Karl. "Hence, the annoying marketing bot that looked just like you."

"Yeah... sorry 'bout that."

"So, what's it like there in the machine?"

"Well, it's not always PG, I can tell you that much. Overall, it's pretty great. It all feels very authentic, at a sensory level. There are programs you can run for different levels of consciousness. There's an amazing app called Dreamtime that I'm kind of hooked on, to be honest. Its tagline is 'If You Can Dream It, You Can Be It.' But when the system gets turned off—like it did—things go black, so that's a definite drawback."

"George, what do you know about the guy they call The One?"

"Oh, *that* dirtbag. I don't even want to—"

And suddenly, Hologram George went dark.

"Someone's turned the power off again," said Karl. "And I have a pretty good idea who it is. Come on!"

And the two of them set off, heading back toward the electrical room near CA1.

As they hurried down the hall, blocks of lights in various sections suddenly went dark.

"Li Yan, is there another path that leads to the electrical

room, other than the corridor leading from the accelerator area?"

She looked at the map. "Yeah, you can take the hallway that leads north just on this side of the Security Checkpoint. There's a door, but it's unlocked. Then take the first left. That'll take you right to it."

"Okay, I'll go that way and take care of the electrical room."

"Hey, look," said Li Yan. "It's Amir!"

"What's going on? The holographic Tour Guide was leading me to you guys when it just disappeared."

"Ya," said Karl, as another corner of the building went dark. "Someone's messing with the power."

"Amir, when we get there, you handle all the same breakers you switched on last time, okay?"

"Don't forget the ones under the desks."

"I won't."

o o o

Storyteller Ceryl was teaching Susan about the wisdom of the spiral path. It was the path to the center of one's self, and the widening path beyond one's limitations. The life journey should embrace both, she said. "Do not fear the challenging path."

"Truth must challenge faith, as surely as doubt must challenge truth. The old is always challenged by the new."

Ceryl told Susan a story in which the High Council were the "old guard" and Susan told a story about a man named Isaac Stern, who was the "old guard" of the MPAS project's executive board.

"In the temple," Susan began, "they worshipped a sleeping god named Anna. In the underworld where the monsters lived, Ada was the mother program. Not everyone realized they were the same thing...."

Susan paused. "Hey, Ceryl, I have an idea for this story...."

"Yes, lover?"

"I'd like to show you the place where I took Kaedra—where the guards claim to have seen the miracle. When you see it, and understand what it is, you'll know the true meaning of Anna."

"Yes, I would like to know."

o   o   o

When Ceryl and Susan arrived at the temple, there were no guards at the door.

Susan opened the heavy wooden door and they stepped inside. Susan led Ceryl up toward the altar and pulled aside the tapestry there. "Climb through here—and be careful. It's very dark down there. I will follow you with this light."

Susan held Ceryl's hands and eased her down through the hatch and then jumped down. As they exited the elevator, a figure moved in the shadows beneath one of the desk consoles. The robed figure stood up suddenly and turned in the sudden glare of Susan's light and Ceryl's look of surprise. "Your Eminence?"

"You should not be here!" he cried, his grimacing face and outstretched hand starkly illuminated by the harsh light.

I know you, realized Susan.

"I know you."

The lights flashed on and seconds later, the accelerator reached peak power. In a ring of light, The One disappeared.

Karl, Li Yan and Amir stepped out of their hiding places around the lab, delighted to see Susan and Ceryl.

o o o

Blink

The One suddenly appeared in a ring of light amid a swirl of dust. His expression of rage suddenly turned to dismay. And there he stood upon the broken platform with his once-proud golden robes flailing in the wind, surrounded by the remains of his fallen temple and a destroyed accelerator. Around him, a horde of curious fish people gathered to poke and prod his wizened right hand. Horrified by their monstrous appearances, he slapped their finny hands away with his younger-looking left hand and cowered amid the rubble.

o o o

As Amir sat waiting for his interview with a New Historian, he pondered what would be the most valuable information he could share. Perhaps the 'Noble Eightfold Path.' Or—much better! —the concept of *pratitya-samutpada*, the inter-dependent arising. The very notion of 'if this exists, that exists; if this ceases to exist, that also ceases to exist' seemed to perfectly summarize the questions in his mind about the path they were about to take.

The historian filed Amir's contributions under Sanskrit,

Buddhism, ancient philosophy, and linked to a previously submission on the concept of dependent origination.

"Thank you, Mr. Roy. We welcome any and all future submissions you may wish to share."

Amir was pleased by the thought that, at this point, Buddhism seemed more aligned with his journey and goals than anything he was seeing in this technological wasteland or the cultish theocracy of those praying to Anna, upstairs.

He wondered if there was a way to share these thoughts with their estranged temple-going neighbors.

He returned to the room where he had spoken with George and called him again. And like a genie, there he was.

"Have your thoughts and philosophies changed," Amir asked him, "since you virtualized here?"

"Oh yes," replied George, performing an ethereal spin. "The reward is in the traveling. We must approach the path to understanding as we do truth: scientifically. If history has taught us anything, it is that things are not always what they seem."

"But knowledge is not understanding, and truth can be subjective."

"Exactly. And the future is not set in stone. We can do our best to determine what is right and what is real; we can calculate the probabilities for the possibilities, but in the end, it is just what we make it."

"Do we dare to ask a question like 'What is the meaning of existence?'"

"Yes, if it is part of our journey toward self-revelation. In our quests for insight and knowledge, we must express our own hearts' needs and desires."

"We all have these questions, don't we?"

"An answer to *that* may suggest pluralistic ignorance, but I dare to believe it so."

"In the world we came from, there seemed to be so little room for faith. But here, I am enriched by it."

"And the world is enriched by you, Amir."

"I would like to find out more about augmentation," said Amir. "Can you help me with that?"

"Yes," said George. "Let me run the orientation program for you."

"Thanks George."

A different voice spoke. "You have enquired about the process known as 'augmenting.' Please note that this process is 100 percent permanent and cannot be undone. You will attain new awareness that cannot be disabled. Your memories will be shared with others on the grid. Are these terms acceptable to you?"

"Yes," said Amir.

After the orientation was complete, the system guided Amir to a nearby room, where a reclining chair with an electronic panel on the headrest awaited him.

"Please place your head comfortably in the headrest area," said the machine as the sides of the headrest extended into a helmet-like apparatus.

"Please relax and remain still and calm while the procedure is underway. This will only take a moment."

An indeterminate amount of time later, Amir's consciousness blinked off and a new one emerged, reborn.

Suddenly, there was a new awareness of the connectedness of all things. The dance of life was—no, *is*—everywhere and tangible in all things—in the microcosm, as life begins; in the moment, extending and returning forever. It is reflected in colors beyond perception, in musical motifs beyond conception, in all forms, as a single grand event—an energy that vibrates the strings that connect all things.

And in all existence, every moment and every thing therein is as one in this continuum, as the dark and the light and all cosmic forces vibrate together in the balance of a perfect harmonic multiverse—a grand helix of all events and things here in the Now.

And as this awareness grows, Amira awakens as if from a dream to see that which is beyond the self, beyond the void, connecting to something previously unseen and unknown. In the cosmic mirror is reflected the Infinite All.

Amira was suddenly aware that Susan was speaking.

"Wake up Amir. Amir!"

Amira's eyes opened.

"What's wrong? Are you okay?"

Was *this* the Susan Amir had known?

Amira smiled. "I see you."

"Why are you connected to this thing?"

So many questions.

The machine withdrew its connections as if by command and Amira embraced Susan. "I did it," he said. "I augmented."

"So, what is it like?"

"It's beautiful."

"Can you be more specific?"

"The specific effects of augmentation include limited physiological changes. I find that my color perception, hearing, touch and other senses have what one might call increased resolution. However, the most apparent effects are psychological in nature. I have a greatly increased sense of empathy for all living things, and a sense of connectedness to all things. I believe these insights are often associated with spiritual concepts. In keeping with these changes, I have decided to change my name—to Amira."

Susan looked worried. "Are you sure you're okay?"

"Never better."

"We need to talk," said Susan.

"So... Amira, huh? Do you consider that a man's name or a woman's name?"

"I no longer think of gender in such simplistic terms. Truth is seldom as simple as a binary system."

I guess 'Amira' is finally coming out, thought Susan. "Well, I'm happy for you. But we do need to talk."

"So, I've decided to stay here," Susan announced. "I like these people, and, well, I've met someone."

"Hmm," said Amira. "This may interfere with an idea that I want to present to you and the rest of the team."

"Oh, don't worry about me. Go ahead and plan whatever you like without me. Please. I appreciate your concern."

"As you wish."

Amira met with Karl and Li Yan and explained the name change and how the continuum was seeking balance. "You're a crazy cat, Amira," said Karl. Li Yan offered a big hug and the offer was accepted.

"I have an idea," announced Amira. "I've been doing some more thinking about that NASA invention that allowed them to send status bits back to the departure point. Assuming that we are able to access the source qubits—which should be recorded as an incoming jump—we could use that to do much more than simply set a few status bits."

"Intriguing," agreed Karl.

"This information would travel on the quantum conduits developed when NASA first sent those entangled qubits forward. We capture those entangled bits and use them to encode a message, and that message is then communicated through to the other partner in the entangled pair. That way, even if *we* can't actually travel backwards through time, the qubits could carry information."

"You know, I think that just might work. That quantum transmission protocol has been a standard research experiment in constant use since the ASTRA project started. It was only interrupted by the Great Fall."

"You do raise a good point," agreed Li Yan. "We *should* be able to communicate with listeners *before* the blackout event. We could warn them about the, uh, 'datapocalypse.' Ick, I hate that term."

Li Yan thought about it for a few seconds. "Yep, that is an awesome idea. We can send a warning back, and really change the world for the better."

Susan was unsure. "Yeah, maybe I've just read too much science fiction, but changing the past never seems to go well. But you know, I think it's an idea worth exploring. And I don't know, but maybe just sending information back wouldn't damage the timeline as much."

"...Or maybe the action we are about to take has always been the cause of our current reality," offered Amira, hopefully.

○ ○ ○

"Cer, you know the story you told of Timeless in The Sun?"

"Yes."

"And I said I thought I knew that story. You said you had another story, about the Elder 'I Am as Time.' I think I know who that is, as well."

"Would you and Kaedra, or any other council member you choose, be willing to accompany me? If you trust me and come with me, I believe we may all gain new insights."

"Is this like a spiritual quest?"

"More like a meditation on the essential nature of all things, I think."

"That sounds good. We think about these things often. I will ask Kaedra to join us."

○ ○ ○

The children sat in a semicircle around the Storyteller as she spoke. "And so it was that the harbingers made contact at last with the god of their children's children and brought their dreams and visions into a new world of knowledge and purpose. And the Council's advisors learned of the ancient ways of Anna, as revealed by the administrators of the ring of wondrous light. With this new awareness, the advisors returned to the Annatarian Council once more in elation, preparing for the dawn of their Second Great Age.

○ ○ ○

Amira spent another day in quiet meditation. Susan was busy with Cer; Karl and Li Yan working in the lab on L1. At last, Amira spoke. "I have been studying the jump records and I have a theory about the origin of the temple."

"I speculate that one or more parties within or associated with the Andna organization had a reason to hate the company or its affiliation with the military. Perhaps he or she was a relative of someone who worked here. I surmise that it may have been this party who guided the self-driving van through the front window of the Andna office building—and was most likely responsible for the subsequent bomb attack on the facility, as well. Certainly, we know that person *did* have access to a transit pod and was able to send a pod full of explosives forward without being inside, which strongly suggests an insider who worked at the company during that period. This narrows the list of suspects significantly. I additionally surmise that this person must have jumped forward shortly before the bombing event (as this was not possible afterward) and either shortly before or after the self-driving van incident, to avoid scrutiny and likely prosecution. I then narrowed the list of jump IDs to this subset and found there were two IDs that met these criteria and had indeed jumped close to both of those events. One was George, but the other one has a particularly interesting pattern of behavior that leads me to believe he or she may be a more likely suspect."

"This monologuing is kind of a new thing for you, Amir. Sorry, *Amira*."

"The individual identified in the records as 'Name not available' made a total of 132 jumps over a period of 400 years, including 130 all exactly four weeks apart during the period in which pod-to-station qubit communications were possible. I believe it was during this period that the temple was constructed here and the Annatarian Council formed. Interestingly, the deed for the land upon which the temple is constructed is owned by Andrew Stern, the son of the first CEO. He did work at both MPAX and Andna and *did* drive a blue van when we first encountered him. I believe that it was Andrew Stern who sent facts back to the past where they became predictions in order to construct the 'prophecies' now associated with the legend of The One."

"So The One *owns* this place? Oops."

"We're probably in a lot of trouble."

"On the other hand, the records show that George was the very last person to use the Jump station."

"Wait—what? *You* were the last person."

"That's not what it says here."

"It's therefore possible that he, with his knowledge of the hardware and operations was an accomplice of the perpetrator."

"But," wondered Li Yan, "if everything points to George, it *could* have been George all along, couldn't it?"

"It seems unlikely that the perpetrator would place himself in as vulnerable a position as George did. He allowed himself to be virtualized into a state where he could easily be deactivated—as he was when we arrived here. He admitted he had given up partial rights to his identity to offset the cost of the virtualization procedure. The true perpetrator, therefore, would be able to use George's persona in this system to carry out various schemes resulting in the records here. Or perhaps coerce George to do it."

"Well, I'm pretty sure that last record was a favor. Thanks George."

"The evidence also suggests that George's ID may have been used at least some of the time by his accomplice as a ploy to incriminate him instead. Indeed, it's possible that George never made the final jump at all, if somehow his face and figure were 3-D scanned and his voice sampled to create a 'deep fake.' It is difficult for us to know—and I'm not certain that even George can be sure at this point."

"Yeah, I'm not sure the real George could pass a Turing Test," sniped Li Yan.

"I heard that."

o o o

21

The Ancients Speak

Karl and Li Yan labored for days to develop a qubit capture system based the NASA example code, with food and moral support provided by Susan and Ceryl the Storyteller. Ceryl suggested that Susan should become a Storyteller and dressed her in traditional Storyteller's garb. "You look very sexy now," she whispered. Amira spent most of the time meditating.

"Okay," said Karl. "I think we're ready. Li Yan's got the revised firmware uploaded and we've got the pod set to sequentially send our warning message back, encoded as ASCII text. It's not very sophisticated, but in this case, its sheer obviousness is the system's key feature. We can only hope they are, if you'll pardon the pun, forward-thinking enough to be looking for incoming data. Here goes."

"What all did you send?"

"I sent two messages, actually. One was a short alert that just repeated over and over and the other was like a short diary, which also repeated. Names, events, dates and times—that sort of thing."

"I have no idea how long we'll have to wait to see a response, but we're just going to leave the qubit timecaster running the messages in a loop. Repeating patterns are the best bet, especially if there's an automated system on the other end."

"Goodnight everybody, great work."

○ ○ ○

Exactly 24 hours later, the Ancients responded. "Message received & decoded. Will take defensive measures. Thanks!"

○ ○ ○

Karl woke up with a start. Beside him in bed was Li Yan with her black hair and blue stripe.

At that exact moment, in his apartment, Amir woke up suddenly, too.

As these things were happening, a raw egg was sliding from a cracked shell in Susan's hand. It hit the pan and began to cook with what looked, just for a moment, like a hint of an egg-white spiral.

Susan realized she must have been daydreaming. She snapped back to reality and looked at the two eggs frying in the pan. Yin and Yang. An odd daydream, she thought.

The phone rang. It was Dr. Rössler.

"Erich! Good morning. To what do I owe this pleasure at such an hour?"

She listened for a moment as he explained.

"From where? What?! Yeah, I guess I'd better. Okay, I'm on my way."

When Susan arrived at the office at 9:01, Karl and Li Yan were already sitting in the conference room. Amir texted to say he was just parking his car.

Rössler explained that the NASA equipment installed at the lab had just received a complex qubit-encoded message. When decoded, it was a message from Karl in the future. Needless to say, Karl in the present was a little surprised to hear this. "Well, apparently, we got past the problems posed by the No-communication theorem and are communicating from the future. I certainly hope it tells us how we end up accomplishing that."

Karl reviewed the message. "It does! It says it was sent via quantum teleportation, but over zero distance."

"Hmm," remarked Li Yan, "I wonder how you are doing that? Using classical communications over the teleportation link, perhaps?"

"Damn. I must've gotten smarter," said Karl with a smile as he reviewed the text. "Hey, you guys are mentioned in this message, too! It seems that we all traveled to the future and somehow or other, we've now forgotten that we were ever there."

"That is truly strange."

"I'm not sure I even want to know my future. And for

that matter, how did we get back here? Logic suggests that we simply haven't left yet."

"I'm not sure if I remember anything about this future path or not. I doubt it's anything like my dreams."

"I don't remember anything, and I'm not prone to feelings of déjà vu. Although there have been a few times...."

"We do have detailed notes, though, which our future selves wisely and kindly thought to include for this very reason."

"Whoa! —It says that the place will be bombed. Twice!"

"When? Maybe we should stop them."

"What—change the past? Hmm—I don't think so. That never goes well."

"Well, it's not the past, it's the present and I think if we can stop a bombing, we should at least try."

"The first bombing is... it says tomorrow."

"When?"

"7:06 a.m."

"Woah. Here?"

"Yeah."

"Damn. I'm taking the day off."

o o o

"Here it comes."

"Let's just block the road and try and not get blown up or run over. If whoever this is can't get into the building, we've accomplished something."

"Watch out! No driver!"

It narrowly missed them as they jumped out of the way.

"Self-driving van wouldn't normally behave that way," observed Karl. "I think its collision and object detection routines have been disabled."

The van drove through the front window.

"Oh my god!"

"No explosion. That's good, I guess."

"Perhaps I made an error in my note. It's possible. Let's have a look. I'd still be careful."

"You don't think it was an accident?"

Karl shook his head as they approached the rear of the vehicle. A manager rushed over and put her hands up. "Sorry—this whole area is closed."

"Can we go upstairs?"

"No, I'm sorry. The whole place is on lockdown. The police are coming." Karl turned as the sound of a siren grew louder. An ambulance pulled into the rotunda out front, just outside the shattered windows.

On the other side of the windows, coworkers surrounded a woman lying in broken glass with a coat on top of her. She was conscious and saw the ambulance crew climb out of the vehicle and hurry toward her. "What happened here?" he asked as he checked her hands for cuts.

o o o

Susan, Karl, Li Yan and Amir watched from the hallway as the ambulance worker knelt down and checked for blood.

"I was hit," she stammered. "Struck down. By this van. Whose van is this? Was there no driver?"

"The police are on their way, ma'am. Are you hurt?"

She sat up. "Ouch."

Karl tapped on the stairwell door. "I'm going downstairs. There's something I want to look at."

"Holy smoke," said Amir, looking at the scene of destruction. "I know this van. This is the one I got a ride in. Andrew's."

Down three flights of stairs they went. A moment later, Karl was examining the logs. "Look at this," he said, pointing to an entry at the top of the list. "'Name not available' was the last person to jump."

"That's weird. That draws more attention than a fake name would."

"Absolutely. It's like he just deleted an ID key. Not really very sophisticated."

"I think we should go tell the police that we know whose van that is," suggested Amir.

Susan thought things through for a few seconds. "And if he's the guy who's missing, don't you think we will have to explain to them?"

"Ya, that's a bad idea. They'll figure it out."

Meanwhile, an officer inspected the interior of the old van. An unusual circuit was wired into the ignition. No registration. And the VIN number had been filed off. Another officer was inspecting the bumper sticker on the rear of the vehicle. Earth First / No plates, he wrote in his book.

"We know for sure that a bomb attack is planned two days from now. Do we know the exact time?"

"Yes, it's supposed to happen at 17:17:17:00. So, July 4, 17 seconds after 5:17 p.m."

"But what can we do? We're no bomb experts. I certainly don't want to be anywhere near it when it shows up."

"What if we have a jump initiated at that exact time, and send it forward again, immediately? Would that work?"

"What? As long as you're not the poor sap who receives it in the future. It's a bit irresponsible to be forwarding bombs, don't you think?"

"It's unlikely that whoever is sending the bomb forward wouldn't wait at least a few seconds before exploding it. That's our window of opportunity. And we don't really have to be present. We can automate that send command with a CRON script."

"Well, I don't want to blow anything up. Can we send it a million years forward or something? As far as possible."

"Ya, I think we can do that."

"I've programmed it to have the field running already at 17:17:16:59. So when the pod gets here at the 17-second mark, it just keeps going."

o o o

They watched the platform from the cam on the ramp deck. At 17:17:17:00, the pod appeared. It did not disappear again. In the corner of the screen, the timer counted the seconds.

"So far there's no evidence we can change the past," observed Karl.

17 seconds later, a message appeared.

Greetings from the brighter world. Trust in a better to-morrow. Translate these messages into other languages and tell others not to fear the future. There is hope.

THE END
of Book One

Recommended Reading

BOOK TWO - HAVEN

Corporatism catches up with a ruthless executive when an AI entity replaces him as CEO of a leading tech company. Meanwhile, his radicalized son and a brilliant programmer steal the world's most valuable intellectual property: a top-secret device capable of communicating with the future. The resulting revelations result in a cult-like following for the mysterious prophet. Is it the beginning of a new world order?

BOOK THREE - HELIOS

Welcome to Seahaven, where an unprecedented solar storm is about to create havoc—and someone has stolen a device capable of communicating with the future. Elsewhere, a top-secret quantum radar program creates a temporal displacement field, but a coding error has far-reaching consequences. With this tech and the knowledge of where and when a disaster known as the Omega Event will occur, the chrononauts attempt to change the future. Or is it inevitable?